AMSTERDAM RAMPANT

NEIL COCKER

CLOUDBURN BOOKS

First published in 2014 by Cloudburn Books

ISBN 978-0-9928329-3-3

http://ncocker.wordpress.com

For Anna

Neil Cocker was born in Scotland in 1972 and lives in Luxembourg with his wife and two rescue dogs. His short stories have won prizes (Canongate 2001), been shortlisted for prizes (Bridport 2010), published in print (New Writing Scotland 21 & 23), and taught on a Scottish Literature course at Oldenburg University.

"What I like about cities is that everything is kingsize, the beauty and the ugliness."

Joseph Brodsky

THURSDAY

The Zip's Teeth

The brothel door needs a coat of paint.

I focus on the brass plaque next to the buzzer – *STRANGE FRUIT*, engraved in flowing script – and wonder if this will be an orgasm too far.

According to the Strange Fruit website, behind this door are dozens of exotic girls and a handful of buff young studs catering to every possible quirk and fetish – "the most fuckalicious experience in Amsterdam". But this is not a fuckalicious door.

I imagine a line-up of all the women in my life – sister, mother, grandmothers, ex-wife, aunts, cousins, colleagues – standing in a long row in the street behind me, silent, gritting their teeth, hair fluffing in the breeze, glowering at the back of my head through narrowed eyes.

Deep breaths. *It's therapy*, I remind myself. Eva assures me she only makes ethical reservations – no trafficked or co-erced workers, just independent sexual entrepreneurs certified to work with sex therapists. What's important is for me to relax and heal myself.

I press the buzzer.

A spurt of static. "Hello?"

My name is Findlay McPhail; people call me Fin. When I'm attending my appointments I go by a different name. "Hi, it's Quincey. I have an appointment at nine."

The intercom drones and the door unlocks. I step into a shadowy hallway. A makeshift reception desk stands at the end of a narrow corridor, and behind the desk, a receptionist. The woman is in her fifties, hair like golden candy floss, lipstick the colour of fresh liver. She speaks to me in a clotted Dutch accent. "Quincey. Appointment at nine. Your reservation is with Zasha, *toch*?"

I shrug. "I think so."

"Two hundred euros cash."

I slide the envelope across the desk. The receptionist untucks the fold, extracts the four crisp fifties, and writes something in her logbook. She hands the empty envelope back to me. "Room 4."

I crumple the envelope into my fist and start walking. The carpet is red and patterned with interlocking white hexagons. The blood's moving faster in my veins now, heating up, swirling with adrenaline and testosterone. I follow the arrow on the wall along the corridor, up a short flight of steps and turn left. Stuff the crumpled envelope into a tube-shaped bin. Room 4 is straight ahead. I pass Room 3 and hear what might be a drill.

My knuckles rap the door to Room 4 – *tat tat tat.*

Movement behind the door.

I hold my shoulders back, try to smile. I think back to that moment when I first met Eva, when she told me I looked like a "friendly goblin." Bluish Celtic skin, short brown hair the texture of steel wool, a crooked broken nose and gappy teeth, and a face that glows like a spanked arse after the gentlest exercise or a few sips of alcohol. Really, I look no worse than most Scottish males.

The door opens, revealing a woman in her early twenties with bobbed black hair, dressed in a red kimono. "Quincey I presume," she says.

"That's me."

"You're my nine o'clock. I'm Zasha." She shakes my hand in her tight little grip and ushers me in. The room is square and cream-coloured: fluffy cream carpet, cream sheets on the bulky bed, cream wallpaper and curtains. Only the pillows on the bed are a different colour, the same deep red as Zasha's kimono. She closes the door with a quiet click.

"So, Mr Quincey," says Zasha. "You live in Amsterdam?"

"Correct."

She smiles playfully. "And what is your line of work?"

"Do you normally ask such probing questions?"

"Pleasantries. Isn't that what it's called?" She toys with the kimono cord, as if considering untying it. "Your therapist told me exactly what you need."

"Really."

"Remove your clothes." Zasha's accent is now taking shape: South American, and going by her European appearance, I would guess Argentinian. My work has taught me much about appearances. She looks half-Latin, half something else, the other half something northern and weird: Finnish or Estonian or Icelandic. Black Latin hair and bleached blue eyes.

I slip off my jacket and kick off my shoes, unbutton my shirt. She crosses the room and takes a heavy-looking bag out the wardrobe. She tosses it onto the bed, and it clinks, gently jostling the bed springs with its weight. Zasha opens the kimono, revealing a sculpted body, nipples like dark berries.

I stand there naked, ready. Zasha beckons me closer and traces a fingernail around the lion rampant tattoo disfiguring my bicep. "Scotland forever," she reads.

"It was a going away present."

She presses her fingernail into my skin – sharp and hard, a reminder who's boss – then turns back to the bed. "First of all you need to put this on. It's important you cannot see what I'm doing."

Zasha rummages in the bag and takes out a black leather mask. I take it from her and squeeze it over my head, trusting Eva. She knows what she's doing, I tell myself, even though her therapy is getting ever more leftfield, ever more uncomfortable.

The mask is tight, has no eyeholes and smells of other people's sweat. The only hole is for my mouth. I see nothing but the blackness of my eyelids. Zasha's fingers fumble with the zip under my chin and pull the mask even tighter, the zip's teeth nipping my neck skin. I push away the feelings of fear and dislocation; dominatrices don't hurt people, I remind myself. It's just about power, nothing else.

"Stage one," she says, her voice muffled. Then her fingers close around my dick, hot and tight, and she guides me onto the bed, the cotton sheets smooth under my knees and hands as I grope my way onto the plateau of the mattress. She nudges me and I lose my balance, roll onto my back. I hear her laugh.

Then something hard and flat smacks into my testicles.

The pain is stunning.

I roar in shock and outrage. Both hands reach between my legs and I curl into a hedgehog ball, cradling the soaring agony, trying somehow to contain it, stop the nausea spilling out through every pore. I uncurl and thrash my fists on the bed, trying to shake away the pain, bicycling my legs jerkily in the air, all the time in leathery darkness, unaware of where Zasha is.

Then the pain shifts: something cold and sharp bites on my right nipple. A yell of shock escapes from my mouth and I grope at my chest and feel some kind of metal clamp digging into my skin. From somewhere to my right, I hear a laugh. I unclip the clamp and release a stinging pain. Panic: soreness and dizziness and darkness make me breathe faster, whimper a little. As I sit up the hard flat thing whacks me on the side of the head, and I fall backwards, rolling across the bed and off the other side in a tumble of elbows and knees. Up and on my feet, survival instincts taking over. I try to make sense of the darkness, imagine the shape of the room. Zasha speaks.

"This is part of the lesson, Quincey. You need to submit. You need to let me win, and I will show you the way to something new."

I reach up to the zip under my chin and tug. It's stuck, snagged on leather and skin. I twist my head to try to free the zip, and at the same moment she hits me again, not quite connecting this time, glancing off my shoulder.

"Stop," I tell her. "Whatever the safety word is, I don't know. I don't care. Just fucking stop."

Zasha's voice, somewhere in the darkness. "Bad boy. I told your therapist the safety word. You're lying."

"No. Fucksake. Stop it. Game over."

A laugh, and another blow, this time a sharp lash on my thigh. A whip.

My hands curl into fists.

"Ohhh, putting up a fight. I like fighters."

In the darkness I am now only aware of the smell of leather and the hammer of my heartbeat. I listen for any noise to help me locate Zasha, bouncing on my toes as if I'm back at the boxing club. But the truth is I've never fought anyone at the boxing club, only done skipping and sit-ups and pummelled a punch-bag. Boxercising is scant preparation for a blind fight with an Argentinian dominatrix.

"Just stop," I tell her. "You can keep the money."

Another lash, this time across my shins. Rage flares up inside and I reach out to grab her, and clutch at air. She laughs again.

Concentrate. I try to listen for her but all I can hear is the rumble of a tram through the double glazing, a distant scream in one of the other rooms. Blackness all around. An image flashes into my head, of playing hide and seek as a child: crammed into an airing cupboard, buried in a smell of cotton and fabric softener, wishing with melancholic abandon that I could spend every day hiding in silent and warm nooks. The image disappears, the smell of sweaty leather harsh again in my nostrils, nausea churning my insides.

I sense movement nearby, a tremble of air against my naked skin, and I lunge forwards in a kamikaze rugby tackle.

A yelp of surprise and my arms pincer around her, sliding at first on the silky kimono, but then clamping around her waist. I drop down to my knees but fight back onto my feet, Zasha wriggling against me, nails tearing into my neck, and I yell at her to stop – *stop, please stop* – but she holds on tight, claws cutting through my skin. Her grip shifts to my windpipe and she begins to squeeze. Dizzy and panicking, I lose my balance and we pitch forwards sharply, thumping into something wooden and hard.

Dizzy blackness.

I become aware that I am lying on something soft. The carpet. I sit up, fumble my way back onto my feet. My hands move to the mask's zip and tug. The zip is still stuck so I twist my head up and pull at a different angle, tearing my skin – but the zip moves a few millimetres. Encouraged, I stretch my head back further, and when I tug again the zip's teeth break open.

I yank the mask off, my sweat-soaked head exposed to cool air, and look at the damage.

Zasha lies unconscious in front of me, the kimono flopped across her, covering her nakedness. By the look of things we rammed the wardrobe. One door hangs off its hinges, revealing a range of costumes hanging on the rail inside: rubber, leather, PVC, chainmail. The carpet by her head is splashed with blood, and the whip lies in the middle of the room like a dead snake.

I crouch down over Zasha and feel for a pulse, fingertips exploring her neck. There is a silver stud shaped like a tiny hand grenade in her earlobe. A gash on her scalp leaks blood, matting her hair. I've never done this pulse thing before, only seen it on the telly, and feel nothing – my heartbeat drowns everything out. *She's dead.* But just as this terrifying thought ricochets around my head, Zasha groans. It's a soft, throaty groan, as if she's talking in her sleep, but she's alive.

I stand up and walk over to the pile of my clothes. I dress quickly, wriggle into my t-shirt and jeans and shrug my leather jacket on. Only one thought now: *get the fuck out of here.*

I take one last look at Zasha crumpled on the floor and gently open the door a couple of inches.

The corridor is empty. I close the door to Room 4 behind me and walk along the corridor. As I pass Room 3 I hear a hysterical laugh and what sounds like a hairdryer. My feet move quickly over the hexagon-patterned carpet: air freshener and spermicide-stink hang in the stillness.

Down the stairs, and towards reception. The candy floss woman is watching a mini TV; tinny laughter and applause echo in the whitewashed hallway.

"Goodbye," I say, three steps from the door.

She calls after me, something in Dutch, and I keep walking.

Cloudburn Calling

Outside, cold wind in my face that already tastes of winter. The door judders shut behind me and I stride up the street, wanting to run but not wanting to be noticed. I head towards the Indonesian restaurant where I chained up my bike. The Overtoom is quiet save for the buzz of an advancing moped and my heart slows a little. But the relief is now replaced with something else. The alkaline taste of dread.

I unlock my bike and wrap the chain around its crossbar. I climb on forgetting about my whacked balls and pain explodes in my crotch; I wobble for a second then raise myself off the seat again and the agony crawls into my bowels and stomach.

After a minute or two – eyes screwed up, teeth sunk into my bottom lip – the pain deadens enough for me to move. I kick off, sitting awkwardly to avoid the pressure of the seat on my nether regions. The wind blows into me hard from the side, wobbling the front wheel.

I bike onto Marnixstraat, cutting out in front of a slowing bus, and pick up speed, my pedalling moving into a steady rhythm. I swing the bike onto a sidestreet, lifting my arse off the seat in time for the rickety jostle of the cobbles. Across the canal, weaving between badly parked cars, the cafes busy, rucks of drinkers clustered round the bars.

I stop pedalling as I turn into Lindenstraat and let the bike wheel to a halt outside my apartment. The pain returns as I dismount, this time from my nipple, chaffing raw against the hem of my jacket. I'd forgotten about the nipple. My hand probes inside my jacket, exploratory, and touches a damp welt. I wince. Some therapy this.

I shut my apartment door firmly behind me, double-lock it and slide the safety chain in place. Home. Or what passes for home in my upside down life: a one-bedroom apartment, paid for by the company, 'luxury' according to the landlord but so sparsely furnished the place looks more like an elegant crack-pad. After a few blissful seconds of darkness and silence I clump up the sheer staircase.

At the top of the steps I flick the lightswitch – the bulb overhead flares and pops, leaving me standing in my living-room in half-darkness. I stay there for a few moments, absorbing the stillness, breathing in the lingering lemongrass smell of the Thai noodles I wolfed two hours ago. In the gloom, the living-room is a moonscape of bulky shapes and outlines, sketched out by the weak streetlight filtering through the curtains.

I hobble across the floor and turn on the reading lamp, splashing a puddle of light onto the laminated wood at my feet. My sofa, thank God for my sofa. I ease down onto its yellow softness, crumple into a foetal position and let a sigh escape.

Tonight's experience was supposed to be a breakthrough: the next leap forwards in my sexual healing. And now, instead of glowing with a post-coital buzz, I'm facing this nightmare weekend with mangled bollocks and a nipple hanging off my chest like a chewed raisin.

I need to phone Eva and find out what the fuck she was thinking, booking me a psycho.

I reach into my jacket pocket for my mobile. My hand slides into an empty space. The pocket is empty.

I grope my pockets one after another – jacket, jeans front and back. And do it again. Nothing. Empty.

I tilt my head back and look up at the ceiling.

I've lost my mobile. And I'm already ninety-nine percent sure it's somewhere in Room 4 next to the unconscious Zasha.

After ten minutes of lying on the sofa – fear eating into me like acid, so nervous I want to puke – the rain beating on the window prompts me to get a hold of myself.

I could call Eva using the landline. I could do that if I knew her number instead of trusting my mobile with every piece of information I need to operate in this city. A brand new Blackberry, upgraded from my old model just last week. I can't even cancel it because all the phone accounts are handled by the departmental secretary. Cancelling it tomorrow will mean admitting it's lost, and I don't even want to think about that at the moment.

I push myself up on my feet, limp over to the wall cabinet and switch on a nearby lamp, illuminating my whisky collection: my life's work. Fifteen bottles glint in the hard light like giant barley sugars, every one of them a different variety of Cloudburn Single Malt Whisky, every one of them designed and marketed by me. I come from a distillery family: my father, grandfather and great-grandfather all worked for Cloudburn. Whisky has both made us and ruined us.

Cloudburn 13 Year Old Single Malt aged in Gran Oloroso cask. I take the bottle and my favourite chunky drinking glass and shuffle back across the floor, pour a healthy dram and place the bottle at my feet.

The landline rings.

I sit and watch as the red light flickers, the shrill ring drilling into the shadows. My brain performs some lightning mental arithmetic: I fled Strange Fruit about forty minutes ago. Zasha woke up and called her pimp thirty-five minutes ago. The psycho-pimp came to her room thirty minutes ago. Found my Blackberry twenty minutes ago. Smiled when he realised it wasn't password protected. Phoned a few people in the address book until he found out exactly who I am, where I live, and what my landline number is.

I let it ring out.

As the room darkens, I wait for the noise of an engine on the street, to be followed shortly by hammering on the door. But all I hear is the rain and the occasional bicycle bell. Maybe it wasn't the psycho-pimp phoning – it could have been my sister Ailsa.

An image comes of her, sitting in the corner of her living-room back in Cloudburn, huddled over the phone, Dingo's snores drifting down from upstairs, their two-year-old boy Calvin sound asleep in the room next to his father. This is what I imagine. But I haven't seen Ailsa, or Cloudburn, for a whole year.

The town is rapidly becoming a figment of my imagination, which is helpful, because marketing whisky is all about myth-making. The real Cloudburn wouldn't sell much whisky to Americans and Japanese, that's for sure. The tour buses only make it to the distillery and back onto the ring road and bypass the town centre. The Cloudburn I grew up in was nothing like the pictures on the website, which make you think that just out of the frame of the photos, bonnie mini-kilted lassies swish past with a sparkle in their blue eyes, Highland cows nibble grass through rickety fences, and legions of tartan-clad townspeople riverdance their way through cobbled streets. It would be much trickier to sell the whisky if I were saddled only with the truth.

I close my eyes and get the guilt. The guilt of the expat. Amsterdam: my new home. But tomorrow a little piece of Cloudburn is coming to Amsterdam: my future brother-in-law Dingo arrives with his stag party entourage. In the silence I clutch my chunky glass in my lap and grit my teeth. As if this current situation couldn't get any worse.

In the apartment next door someone drags furniture across the wooden floor. The TV downstairs screeches and wails. My balls hurt.

Two gulps and the whisky is gone. I pour myself another, then hobble up the spiral staircase to my bedroom, footsteps clunking on every step. At the top of the stairs I glance out the porthole window into my neighbour's attic living-room – a mere two metres away – and see him hunched over dinner, scooping meat stew into his mouth. He caught me staring last week and gave me the finger.

I rock on my feet, too much whisky too soon, fully in contradiction of the company's responsible drinking policy, but it's taken the edge off the pain. I open the bedroom door with a nudge of my foot.

On the windowsill above the bed is the Dictaphone and a landslide of blank tapes. This is what's caused all the trouble. The next blank tape is waiting to be filled with the details of tonight's disaster. I wonder if the police will find the tape next to my dead body.

I empty the glass into my mouth – the liquid trickles between my gums and bottom lip, and I suck it back up over my tongue, swirl and swallow. Cloudburn: the whisky in my blood, forever in my blood.

FRIDAY

Extracted from www.cloudburn.com

Nobody had ever set foot in Fairy Glen and survived – or so the locals claimed.

Legend had it the only light ever witnessed in this dark entanglement of trees, ivy and thornbushes was when the fairies threw one of their demonic ceilidhs: on those rare occasions, dancing torches were spotted flickering through the trees, accompanied by an unearthly din of discordant fiddles, pummelling drums and howls echoing around the hillsides. For hundreds of years the fairies were left alone to their devices in this scrap of woodland on the edge of the Scottish Highlands – until 1889, the year that Cloudburn Distillery was built.

Brothers James and Edward Skene, industrialists and heirs to the lands of the county, decided that in this age of modernity it was time to overcome local superstition and bring the glories of commerce to this forgotten corner of Scotland. First they employed a gang of navvies to slash and burn their way through the glen. For many weeks the hillsides glowed from their fires, and slowly, yard by yard, half of the glen was cleared by the Irishmen to make way for the distillery. The site was highly satisfactory – level, sheltered, and positioned closely to the water source of MacLeod's Burn. Perfect, as far as the Skenes were concerned. But the locals saw it differently, and believed that the brothers were undoubtedly cursed for violating the fairies' domain.

For the next twenty years, the Skenes could do no wrong. First, they named their distillery 'Cloudburn', in mischievous honour of James's childhood inability to pronounce 'MacLeod's Burn'. Edward was a skilled chemist and applied his knowledge and abilities to crafting a whisky of outstanding quality. James had a head for numbers and a way with people. A town grew up around the distillery, and Cloudburn's fine malt spirit was supped in outposts of the empire by eminent colonialists. But the downfall of the Skenes was just around the corner. Their young sons, cousins yet more like brothers, went to play in the remaining woods of Fairy Glen one blustery November day. They disappeared without trace.

Every day for two weeks, search parties hacked through the thicket to search for the distillery's missing heirs. As the first snows advanced over the Ochils the searchers discovered two pairs of children's shoes dangling from a jagged briar. In whirling snow, the search was abandoned.

The Skene brothers were inconsolable, and blamed each other for the loss of their sons. As the years passed and no further heirs were forthcoming, their feud grew increasingly bitter. The family mansion split into separate wings. The brothers refused to work at the distillery on the same day. Business began to suffer, and in the summer of 1928, Edward Skene took to bed with stomach pains. The doctor diagnosed cancer, and within weeks he had wasted away to a skeleton. But Edward's final act was a noble one – he presented his brother with a bottle of Cloudburn from the first ever cask distilled, and pleaded for his brother to drink a dram from this ‘Bottle of Brotherhood’ every new year, and remember everything they had achieved together – and remember too their poor lost sons. Edward died the next day.

James would not live long enough to open the bottle. A few weeks later he was found with his head split open on the distillery road, having apparently slipped on black ice. He lay in a coma for three months and passed away in the first days of 1929. The distillery was sold off, and the Skene family was consigned to history. In the hostelries of Cloudburn the locals muttered again of the fairies’ curse.

Today, the remainder of Fairy Glen is a wild thicket untamed by human hand – overgrown, shadowy and impenetrable. At Cloudburn Distillery we intend to leave it that way. Just like our distilling methods, we believe some things in life should never be meddled with.

Newt Sarkissian

Someone batters on the front door. Thump. Thump thump thump. I lurch upright, swaying in the gurgling swamp of my waterbed, expecting at any moment to hear the sound of wood splintering.

But the noise isn't coming from the front door – it's the window behind me, the North Sea wind jiggling the glass in its frame.

I sit slouched on the bed, waiting for my pulse to calm. Grey morning light leaks through the curtains and pigeons coo on my windowsill. He will come today. For sure the psycho-pimp will come today. I go for a shower.

On the bike ride to work everything makes me jump. Windblown leaves scatter across the bike paths like swarming mice. Bicycle bells reverberate in my bones. At Willemsbrug the traffic barriers drop down – red light flashing and klaxon trilling – and the canal bridge splits in the middle, the two halves cranking up skywards. A couple of minutes later three barges laden with hillocks of gravel ghost silently by, churning the brown water into foam. Out the corner of my eye I sense people watching me: smoking on their bikes, peering out of car windows, scowling over from the pedestrian crossing.

By the time I reach my desk it's nine o'clock. Half the pods in the open plan office are already occupied. I dock my laptop and as the new emails tumble into my inbox, I notice that I have a meeting at nine-thirty with my boss, the wonderful Newt Sarkissian. Fuck, I'd forgotten.

My phone rings. The caller ID shows it's my mother.

I take a deep breath and lift the receiver. "Hi, mum."

"I'll hi-mum you," she says.

"I thought you'd be glad to hear the voice of your only son–"

"Well, ye might no be my son for much longer if ye dinnae look after Dingo this weekend. I'll disown ye if he comes back wi tattoos or an itchy crotch. If he comes back wi a black eye I'll gie ye one myself."

"Stop being over-dramatic–"

"No sex shows, right? N keep him away fae McDonalds, he needs tae fit intae his kilt next week."

I pinch the bridge of my nose between finger and thumb. "Mum, cmon. I'm a grown man. A responsible adult."

"Well, I dinnae ken about that. Ye cannae even look after a mobile phone, never mind yir future brother-in-law."

Ice in my guts.

"Mobile phone?"

"Aye – mobile phone. I got a call last night fae a nice man who found yir phone in a bar. I gave him yir home address. He says he'll pop roond tae yir hoose n return it."

Already, I have an image of this nice man: chunky rings like knuckledusters, dull eyes, face a patchwork of scar tissue. My hand tightens on the receiver.

"So whit have ye got planned for them the night?"

I imagine the psycho-pimp waiting outside my apartment this evening, peering up at the first-floor windows, looking for signs of life. Smiling to himself, fingering the cosh in the inside pocket of his jacket.

"A few pubs."

"None eh that wacky baccy, right?"

"Uh-huh."

"Look after yirself son: n Dingo too. Remember yir sister n aw her troubles doon the years: this is her day. Her chance eh bein happy. Ye dinnae want tae take that away fae her, do ye?"

"No."

Silence down the line, and I know that both of us are thinking the same thing.

"Bye Fin. Call me tomorrow, OK?"

"Aye mum. I promise you I'll look after him."

She hangs up.

Voices at the coffee corner, the whirring beat of the photocopier: I am dimly aware of these noises from another world. It takes a couple of minutes for my heartbeat and breathing to regulate. I am fucked. At least the psycho-pimp doesn't know where I work. Small mercies.

I click open a new email and type **Eva Rosie** in the address bar. In the title bar, I opt for a header of **WHAT**

THE F*CK WERE YOU THINKING??? and underneath I write:

Eva

*Why did you book me a psychopath? Don't give me the broaden your horizons crap, this wasn't part of our deal. This crazy Argentinian attacked me. And now the f*cking pimp is after me. What happened to gently helping me overcome my problems with intimacy?*

We need to talk. This is not therapy, this is torture. Call me at work (I lost my mobile) or email me back ASAP.

Your faithful guinea pig
Fin

I go for a walk to help me calm down: a lap of the office. On my way back, I stop at the display cabinet and peer at the rows of bottles safely locked behind glass.

The Cloudburn is tucked away in the bottom corner, almost hidden behind a promotional gift carton for Sproat's Botanical. Dark green and dusty, the bottle is turned away slightly, the front label only half-showing, as if trying to hide. I crouch down the side of the cabinet so I can stare the label in its face.

The Bottle of Brotherhood. The label has faded to the colour of tea-stains, and a couple of centimetres of liquid have evaporated through the cork in the last hundred and fifteen years. This bottle is the only one of its kind left in the world: said to contain spirit from the first ever batch of whisky distilled in Cloudburn in 1893, part of Scotland's heritage, and beyond price on the collector's market. A bottle given from one Cloudburn distillery owner to the other on his deathbed, a final act of reconciliation after decades of arguments and conflict.

Once, this bottle was in its own display case – the centrepiece of the Cloudburn visitor centre. I lean close to the cabinet, breath misting the glass. A pang of homesickness hits me, before morphing into another bad feeling. *Strange Fruit.* The psycho-pimp will come for me today.

When I return to my desk and unlock my laptop, an email from Eva ghosts into my inbox.

RE: WHAT THE F*CK WERE YOU THINKING?

Fin

I think this latest incident shows that my hands-on therapy is not for everyone. Some people are beyond helping – a therapist just has to accept that fact sometimes. Let's close things down and call it quits.

Goodbye
Eva

I read it again. And a third time.

On screen, the pop-up flashes. Ten minutes till the meeting. I click snooze.

Newt arrives, coughing, clearing his throat, barking hello at people. I watch him as he slings down his bag, throws off his jacket, wriggles a hand into his armpit, scratches for a few seconds, and then sits down with a whimpering sigh. “Friday,” he announces. “Then it’s a whole two days with the wife and kids.”

From my desk I can watch Newt without him noticing. He takes a folder out of his bag and opens it, riffs through some papers, finds what he’s looking for, then turns to his PC. He cracks his knuckles one by one, rolls his head, and stretches his shoulder muscles as if limbering up for a fight. Not a good sign.

After five years of growth, Cloudburn sales have slid dramatically month-on-month since the summer. There was a time when a meeting with Newt Sarkissian meant praise and back-slapping and talk of great things to come. When I moved to Amsterdam a year ago, I came with a reputation. I was the man who had single-handedly saved Cloudburn Single Malt Whisky from extinction. I was the golden boy.

Back in those halcyon days I even had the honour of a night out with him. One evening my doorbell rang, and outside a black Chrysler taxi waited in the narrow street, engine running. Newt stood with one hand on the taxi’s roof, frowning up at the black sky. *Let’s go for drinks*, he said.

We zig-zagged over the canals, Newt talking about the Stalwart share price while I looked out the window, bikes whizzing past, canals shimmering with liquid reflections. The driver dropped us on the edge of the red-light district and Newt grabbed my jacket sleeve and tugged me close, told me he was gonna show me some of the sights.

We drank beers with whisky chasers in tacky bars as Newt told me about everything he'd achieved – *against all the odds, my friend, against astonishing odds* – while I nibbled on rice crackers and asked him questions in the right places. Yes, he thought the acquisition of Cloudburn was a big step for the company. Yes, the opportunities were there for career growth: he himself planned to be CEO of Stalwart within five years. More whiskies, Newt's eyelids beginning to droop.

He went silent and gripped my shoulder, thumb digging into the bone, and told me he was going to take me somewhere special. Out into the dark winter night, I followed him down an alleyway to a door, and he slipped the bouncer some cash. It was still early, and the place was empty, so we sat at the bar, an illuminated catwalk with dancing poles. The barmaids were topless. Girls came out from a side door and climbed up onto the bar, peeled off their bikini tops and thongs and spiralled above us. Newt paid for three lap-dances, each time ordering a tequila shot and paying extra to lick salt and lime juice off the breasts of the dancer. This is the image burned indelibly into my memory: Newt, his face buried in silicone cleavage like a pig in a trough, eyes meeting mine as his tongue squirmed over a nipple.

Pop-up flashing. It's time.

Newt stands, picks up the folder off his desk. I follow him over the carpet tiles and into the meeting room.

He presses a button on the wall and the blinds roll up. Weak autumn sunlight leaks into the room. "Your father works at Cloudburn distillery, right?"

"Huh?"

"Your father. He works at Cloudburn? And your brother?"

"Brother-in-law. Well, future brother-in-law."

Newt sighs. "A family tragedy."

I sit down.

Newt presses his fingers into his forehead. "When we recruited you last year, you know what I decided? To let you do your own thing. Your record spoke for itself. I never liked all the spooky shit – distillery family cursed by fairies etcetera – but it sold. Somehow it sold."

A loaded pause, and then he continues. "What happened at *Amsterdram*? I heard some rumours."

I was worried this would come up. "A blip."

I hit rock bottom last month at the biggest whisky festival in Benelux. *Amsterdram*, it's called – a two-day extravaganza hosted every September in the Oude Kerk. Around fifty stalls showcasing scotch and world whiskies, nosing and tasting sessions, bagpipers, red-headed models dressed in mini-kilts, and the unique opportunity for consumers to buy mutton pies, ultra-sweet fudge, branded golf balls, and tartan gonks.

I gave a presentation on Cloudburn whisky. The hubbub in the church grew as I talked, and I became aware of the audience up close, their faces showing little emotion. I saw two well-known Scottish whisky writers talk to each other and laugh. Coloured light filtered through the stained-glass windows, a pigeon flapped between the rafters high above. I experienced an out-of-body moment: five seconds of dizziness, vision darkening to blood-red. A sharp intake of breath and I was back in Cloudburn, standing on the rocky hillside, MacLeod's Burn gushing past me. Water darkened by moorland peat, soon to be locked into copper stills and transformed into alcohol. A moment of silence in the hubbub, and my disembodied thumb pressed the gadget in my disembodied hand. The next slide flicked up on screen.

I fucking bombed.

Newt opens a bulging manila folder and my career spills out. Six years of marketing and advertising materials: the holographic evil fairy magazine ads, the monochrome posters with the strapline *A Whisky to Die For*, the ads we ran at the Comic Conventions. And also, it shocks me to see, some of the rare and valuable content from the Cloudburn archives, which is supposed to be safely locked up in the vault of an Amsterdam bank as part of the brand ownership contract.

A sepia print of the famous fairy photo, spored with age. One half of the picture shows the furthermost distillery building, a red-brick edifice disfigured by white acetate blobs. The other half of the photo still sends a chill through me after all these years: a tiny human form, smudged by motion, moving towards the bramble bushes at the fringe of the photo. At first glance it could be a child, but closer inspection reveals that this is no child. A hat, boots, and a beard. Spooky as hell.

An independent photographic expert verified the picture's authenticity but made the point that the "fairy" could in fact be a midget. I kept that quiet during the marketing campaigns.

Other highly rare material peeks out from the pile. An original label from the 1920s, its red text proclaiming Cloudburn to be *The Gentleman's Choice*. A postcard I salvaged from a backstreet Glasgow antique dealer showing a kilted soldier relaxing with a glass of Cloudburn while a brown-skinned man in turban and loincloth buffs his shoes. *EMPIRE'S No.1*, alleges the slogan. Another postcard: a moustachioed man in vest and khaki trousers stands with one foot resting on a dead tiger. In his hand he holds a glass of whisky aloft with homoerotic jauntiness. The slogan: *OVERCOME ALL WITH CLOUDBURN*.

The bundle of bumph looks deliberately crumpled and past its sell-by. All part of Newt's performance.

"I'll tell it to you quick," he says. "Sales have been in freefall for the last four months. The board has advised an urgent new direction."

"How urgent?"

"Monday. I need a killer concept, Findlay. It's not just your career you're trying to save here, it's the distillery too. Am I clear?"

"What?"

"Cloudburn is the Betamax of the whisky world. One last chance. Monday."

There are only seventy-two hours between now and Monday morning.

"And if I don't come up with a killer concept?"

Newt frowns. "Findlay, you are here on an expat contract. We pay you a good salary, your rent, other expenses. The company spends a lot of money on you, and at the moment it's not getting much back. Do I have to spell it out for you?"

It's starting to sink in. I try to speak but nothing comes out.

Newt is staring at my chest.

"You're bleeding," he says.

I glance down. A bloodstain the size of a penny has spread on the left breast pocket of my blue shirt.

Newt looks at me, holding my gaze for a few seconds. "You have a great track record with the company, that's why I'm giving you one last chance."

He leaves the room.

I close my eyes and wonder what to do. Is there anything I can do? My thoughts stray to Dingo – probably on his first pint at Edinburgh Airport right now, laughing with his boozehound, druggy friends, all of whom wish to celebrate his impending nuptials by drinking, smoking, snorting and screwing everything they can get their hands on.

I unbutton my shirt halfway down and peer inside at my mangled nipple. A bead of blood collects near the tip, waiting for vampires.

Test Tape

[noise of scratchy static, the microphone rubbing against something]

Right, Eva. You said I should practise talking into the Dictaphone before we really get down to this therapy business. You told me I should get comfortable speaking about all the stuff I don't want to speak about.

So here I am, talking to myself. A practice tape.

A tape I definitely won't be sharing with you.

[muttering, and a sigh]

I'm in my bathroom, sitting on my washing machine, drinking a can of lager. I like sitting here because I can look out the window onto Amsterdam's rooftops. It's almost midnight and the city is still: lights are slowly turning off, leaving black rectangles in the old townhouses. From up here, I can see how the buildings have changed down the years – cement seams where extensions have been added, rickety screwed-on balconies, roofs re-tiled in different shades of red slate. Beyond the buildings, I can see the spire of the Westerkerk, spotlit and golden. It's right next to the

Anne Frank house, and if I remember correctly she would listen to its bells ringing.

It's October 2008, and I've lived in Amsterdam for one year. Before this, I lived in Scotland for all of my thirty-something years, and this is what I don't want to talk about. So I'll start by talking about Amsterdam.

I organised the job transfer here back in the early autumn of 2007. It all happened quickly. In the weeks that followed I packed up my life in Scotland and tried not to think about everything that had gone wrong. Unsuccessfully, of course. I saw my ex-wife once: I was on a bus going round the corner at Haymarket and she was waiting at the pedestrian crossing – our eyes met briefly through the window and slid away from each other again, a brief intersection of past lives.

My old pal Dingo couldn't make it through to Edinburgh for my farewell party but turned up the day after. Lunchtime, the intercom buzzer tore into the silence, and there he was, with bacon rolls and a six-pack. I was hungover, still in my dressing gown. We ate our rolls, polished off the beer, and jumped in a taxi. He gave the driver directions to a tattoo parlour on Leith Walk. I protested to Dingo, he protested back. *We've both got an appointment*, he said, as if that made it okay.

I had never entertained the idea of a tattoo in the past, but at that precise moment – fuzzy-headed as the taxi swung corners, impending emigration like the end of the world looming – I decided to go with whatever he had planned. Two hours later we sat in the Cask & Barrel, arms bandaged, sipping Guinness. Retro lion rampants inked on our skin, accompanied by – at

Dingo's insistence – the legend 'Scotland Forever'. *That's us barcoded now*, he said.

And so I left.

On that first day in Amsterdam I felt like Dorothy in Oz, transported from monochrome to technicolour. A taxi took me from the airport into the city and edged along the canals deep into the Jordaan until reaching my apartment. I headed out to explore the neighbourhood just as it was getting dark. Strings of lights on the old canal bridges dripped orange reflections onto the water. The bars were a hubbub of warm sepia colours. I found a Thai restaurant near my new home and ordered some takeaway. I watched the staff throwing handfuls of ingredients into woks and scraping these bits of green and red around as flames licked the sides of the pot. I walked home past the rows of gabled houses, the occasional bicycle bell pinging through the autumn quiet. And back at my new flat, which smelled of dust and other people, I opened the takeaway by poking my thumbs through the plastic bag. Red chillies and green beans that squeaked against my teeth, chicken that tingled in my mouth with lemongrass and ginger. The food tasted of a new life.

I had big plans for a fresh start. I joined a gym and started boxercising. I bought a bike and cycled to work every day. I went to cafes in the evening and drank mint tea and flicked through the pages of university brochures for MBA distance learning. At the office I worked long hours with the lawyers to transfer Cloudburn brand ownership over to the new company. A slow realisation crept in – my job had been dumbed down. I spent the next few weeks working with a Lithuanian temp to transfer brand data and upload Cloudburn's artwork into Stalwart's product data system. Long days ticking through lists as screeds of Cloudburn artwork files were converted into PDFs and loaded up into the system so that account managers in Miami or Singapore or Buenos Aires could view product artwork at a double-click. The temp didn't show up one day, or the next, leaving nothing behind except his door pass and an empty pack of cigarettes. As snow whirled down on Amsterdam, the data entry tasks fell on my head, and I ended up working over Christmas to meet the legal deadline for January 1st. Keyboard rattling as I sat in the empty office, hooked up to my iPod, typing in product numbers. Whisky had always meant a kind of mystery to me: silent men in blue overalls walking between vats, sheets of rain falling on old buildings, the alchemy of air and water converting to spirit. Now it was a different sort of mystery.

Perhaps this befuddlement led to my downfall.

A bitter January Saturday: cobbles grouted with frost, skin of ice on the canals, and a savage wind. I was on my way to visit the Van Gogh Museum. But halfway down Prinsengracht I glanced up an alleyway and spotted a Saltire billowing from the side of a building.

A Scottish pub. The façade made up of planks of dark varnished wood and the ends of whisky barrels ramshackled together, the pub's name – The Nova Scotia – carved in black Celtic script on pine. Two windows revealing little of the insides other than the blue glow of a plasma TV. Next to the lacquered door a glass-encased sheet of A4 paper displayed the menu: Full Scottish Breakfast, Ayrshire Bacon on a Morning Roll, Haggis Neeps & Tatties served with Whisky & Oatcakes, Stovies & Gravy, Grilled Salmon & Chips, Battered Fish & Chips, Chicken & Chips, Cheeseburger & Chips. I loitered for a few seconds, and then decided to have a pint to warm myself up.

The interior was an eye-watering stramash of clashing tartans: green and blue pinstriped tablecloths; red, black and orange wallpaper. Framed pictures of B-list Scots hung on the walls. Antlers dangled from the rafters.

A man with straggly black hair stood behind the bar, frowning into the distance, arms planted in front of him. Callum MacBean, the landlord. The lone punter sat opposite, a chubby Northern Irish guy with a half-beard. Drew Morrow. My new best friends. I stayed in the pub for eight pints, listening to Morrow rattling on about Amsterdam's freedoms and sins.

The Nova Scotia became a gateway drug, opening me up to further vices. I started going three or four times a week. MacBean knew how to hook me: cask eighty shilling from a small Perthshire brewery, free oatcakes and cheddar, cheery piss-taking and random banter. It became a refuge from the pile of admin at the office. It was a thrill to get on my bike after work and bomb through Westerpark, swishing through parkland and on through sidestreets and canals, until I could freewheel my way towards the dangling flag.

MacBean tolerated cannabis at quiet times, and once we got the nod Morrow would roll skinny joints and we would smoke and drink until we could no longer talk or think. Jukebox belting away, usually Del Amitri or Hipsway or other Jocktastic singalong, clinking glasses and watching the puggie lights shift and shimmer.

Sometimes on those headache mornings at work I would think about my ex-wife Kathleen. I would imagine her in our old flat living her detoxified life of meditation and mineral water, Hamish praying next to her with his trimmed beard and hiking trousers with zip-off legs. Those pictures would creep into my head along with the hangover but I could banish them with hard work and strong tea. And anyway, I'd console myself, there were worse vices in Amsterdam than a fondness for a few beers. In my forays onto the expat scene I'd always been surprised at how often the respectable bankers or IT consultants I spoke to would be telling me by pint four all about the prostitutes they'd slept with, or the darkrooms they'd been in. For a boy from smalltown Scotland it was a shock to hear what went on: the endless availability of tits and pills and powders and cocks and holes. At least I wasn't one of these lost boys stumbling between neon basements. I was just a lonely lush.

On a Saturday night in July, nine months into my Amsterdam life, I was entrenched at the bar with Morrow. We were both enjoying the peace and quiet before his Surinamese girlfriend Esther turned up. She came along to the pub mostly to berate him for his slothful alcoholic lifestyle while quaffing glass after glass of white wine herself.

MacBean was keeping the pints flowing in our direction. He also had an active love life, working on a bisexual rota, dating women one month and men the next. He was incapable of keeping his sex life private and would spend a couple of hours huffing and sighing behind the bar until blurting out his current dilemma, which inevitably resulted in Morrow deriding him as a pervert and a slut. This was always followed by a five-minute shouting match until MacBean threatened to close the pub early, and Morrow of course shut his mouth.

I always avoided talking about my sex life, or more specifically the lack of it, until MacBean broke the silence on the subject and asked me who or what I had sex with.

I told them I wasn't sure anymore – it had been more than a year.

Are you fockin serious? Morrow said.

I told them I didn't feel like it at the moment. The truth was it felt like someone had pillaged my library of sexual thoughts and feelings, emptied the encyclopaedias off the shelves into skips and towed it all away, leaving nothing but vacant corridors and skeletal racks.

Morrow coughed, some kind of embarrassed reflex, and I was aware of him and MacBean smirking at each other: *Someone who doesn't have sex – how fucked up is this?*

I still remember MacBean's words. *We all have our reasons for being who we are.*

The next day I got an email from MacBean saying that he'd thought of an old friend I would click with. Attached to the email was a photograph of a smiling brunette sitting at a cafe table, *This is Lindy* typed below. She was cute. MacBean said Lindy was American and had a thing for Celtic men and was pretty sure he could set up a blind date: all I needed to do was call.

I spent some time that evening looking at a printout of Lindy's photo. It was hard to remember the process and emotions of going on a date. I tilted the photo at various angles to try and ascertain the colour of her eyes, the length of her legs, the size of her breasts. And then I spent some time looking at myself in the mirror: my thinning hair, my grey skin, my empty eyes.

I rang MacBean the next day. He spoke quietly, bar noise in the background, and said he'd fix me up. She emailed. I was to meet her at seven o'clock on Friday at 15 Canada Laan. It was where she worked: if I just asked for Lindy then someone would show me where to go. She signed her email off with a line that made me queasy with possibility. *We can go get some apple pie, I know a great place. Lindy. Kiss kiss kiss.*

That night I lay awake, the shadows moving across the bedroom wall as dawn filtered into morning, a feeling of pure and condensed loneliness so thick in the room I could almost breathe it.

[noise of beer can opening]

The next day I left work early, leaving plenty time to get changed and bike to Canada Laan, which the A-Z showed was in the heart of the red-light district. Ironic after my stint of celibacy, but this twist made the idea appeal even more. What was the worst that could happen? That there would be no mutual attraction? A couple of drinks with an intelligent and attractive woman would surely be a more positive experience than sitting in The Nova Scotia watching Morrow balancing peanuts on his nose.

Forty-five minutes later I was biking towards the red lights. As I turned onto Zeedijk I dismounted and wheeled my bike through the crowds of tourists, peering down the sidestreets for Canada Laan. I was about to retrace my steps when I saw it: a narrow, darkened alleyway, the sign squiggled with graffiti. The mouth of the alleyway broadened into a throat, and by the time I found number 15, it had widened out enough to accommodate a bicycle rack. I chained up my bike next to a small tree and opened the door.

The building seemed to be some kind of sports or dance hall. I stepped into the vestibule, which smelled of cheesy feet, Deep Heat spray and varnish. The polished wooden hallway stretched for a full ten metres and ended next to adjacent signs for the male and female dressing-rooms. I stood absolutely still until I could make out the murmur of voices – several of them – behind a door on my right. Pinned to the door was an A4 sheet bearing the acronym **T.A.G.** I knocked once and entered.

It was a small room. In the middle of the wooden floor, a huddle of people sat in a rough circle on plastic chairs. They all looked at me like I was interrupting.

A woman dressed in a multi-coloured sari – or shawl, I wasn't sure to be honest – stood up and grinned at me. She said: *You must be Fin.*

I'm like: *Aye. I'm looking for Lindy?*

That's me, she said. This wasn't the Lindy from the photograph. This Lindy was in her fifties and not particularly athletic.

Welcome, she said, waving me towards an empty chair.

I started protesting and she told me not to be shy – take a seat.

Perplexed, I did as she suggested. I made for the empty chair and sat down too heavily: the legs shrieked against the wooden floor.

Lindy turned her eager smile on me again. *Can you please introduce yourself and tell us why you decided to join The Amoeba Group.*

I'm thinking: *The Amoeba Group? What the fuck?*

Fin McPhail, I said, and then after a pause, *I came here because I thought it was time I got out a bit more.* In the expectant silence my voice sounded more Scottish than usual.

Welcome Fin, said Lindy, face frozen in a sympathetic grin. *Howsabout we all introduce ourselves to Fin and make him feel at home? And tell him something about why we're all here? Michael, do you want to start?*

The man sitting to her left tilted his head in my direction. *Welcome Fin. I'm Michael, originally from South Africa. I emigrated to Amsterdam in 1992. I thought I was gay and lived a promiscuous gay lifestyle for around ten years, before turning my back on sex. And now I'm asexual, and finally happy with myself.* He nodded at me serenely.

Next was a small dark-haired woman with sleepy half-closed eyes and a droning voice.

Welcome Fin, I'm Candy from Missouri. I have never had sexual relations with anybody in my life and long may that continue.

A scatter of chuckles.

Next. *My name is Peter and I come from Amsterdam. I was married for five years but the relationship with my wife deteriorated because she had a very high sex drive and I had none. Ever since...*

At this point, I noticed movement through the window. The tree where I'd chained up my bike was wobbling frantically. Maybe a hurricane would save me from whatever was happening. But it was no hurricane: a couple of seconds later a hand appeared on an upper branch, and the top half of Morrow's head edged into view.

An asexual group. Morrow and MacBean: it all made sense now. A photo of one of MacBean's pals, a fake hotmail address... the tree wobbled again and MacBean's head edged into view. Bastards.

Peter was still waffling away: ... *and that's really why I chose to turn my back on pleasures of the flesh, as you native speakers say!*

The chuckling brought me back into the room: I glanced towards the door and back to Lindy. I was about to bolt for it when the next person started speaking.

You, Eva.

Hi, I'm Eva Rosie, from Australia but my father is Dutch so I have roots here. You were smiling at me. Your hair cut in a sharp bob, dressed in a tight-fitting red tracksuit with white stripes running down the arms and legs. *I'm not an asexual*, you said. *I'm a sexologist, here as a guest.*

Lindy started talking about her own background, New York and an abusive lesbian lover, but I was still staring at you. You were doodling on a notebook, and as I stared, telepathically willing you to look back, you stopped scribbling and gazed directly at me. I smiled. You smiled back.

As Lindy waffled on, I couldn't stop looking at you. Glance, look away, and repeat. A startling image came to me as I returned my gaze to the floor: of unpeeling your red tracksuit and burrowing my head between your smooth-skinned legs. I closed my eyes, imagining your thighs clamping tightly onto my ears, the others watching. It was no longer possible to get up and run for it because I had my first erection in public for more than a year.

Lindy waffling: ... *and after the hysterectomy, I needed a new life, so I moved to Amsterdam. And in this city I truly realised my sexual identity. I am asexual. An amoeba. And I wanted to meet others like me, so I started T.A.G.*

A moment of respectful silence, Lindy's fingertips pressed together in a pyramid.

What about you, Fin? Lindy's face eager, imploring me. *Tell us your story.*

I shuffled on the plastic chair, buttocks slipping on its polished surface, and hid my erection under my shirt-tail. I said that I didn't really want to talk about it.

Lindy nodded. *We understand. It's difficult to talk at first. But let me guess – you feel excluded from a society which sees somebody not having sex as a failure, right? In a city where sex is constantly shoved in your face, you feel that you need to find a space where you can truly be yourself? With people the same as you?*

I glanced over at you, and you widened your eyes, urging me to agree.

Yes, I said. *I feel very excluded.*

Lindy gave me a tight-lipped smile. *You're in the right place, Fin. Now, this week Candy has agreed to tell us in more detail about how she de-sexualised her apartment.*

After twenty seconds of Candy talking about her unique hybrid of aromatherapy and neutral colour schemes my erection drooped. Ten minutes later we broke for coffee. I waited until you got out of your chair and joined you at the back of the queue.

I came out with a crap chat-up line: *So out of all the ologies to choose from, you went and picked sexology.*

You laughed.

I asked what your speciality was, and in a quieter voice you told me you were focusing on shock therapy, the idea that sexuality can be learned, programmed, deprogrammed. You whispered to me: *Don't tell the others.*

I asked if you were like one of those nutters in the US that try to cure homosexuality.

You looked pissed off.

You told me more. *I'm working on the theory that all sexuality is fluid, and with the right guidance it can flow in any direction. With asexuals, I think it's just that their sexuality has been scared away into the depths of their subconscious. Is that what happened to you?*

I said that surely we all experience peaks and troughs throughout life.

You said that the group was full of quitters, and that you thought I subconsciously wanted proof that I'm not ready to give up on sex yet.

I said it was a bit more complicated than that.

The room was noisy – the Amoebas clearly knew each other well, and there was a bit of a party atmosphere, several loud conversations going on at once. On the chipped Formica table, a choice of coffee or fruit tea in transparent pots. I took two polystyrene cups and asked you what you wanted.

Tea. And to get to know you better.

My hand shook as I poured.

You said I seemed *conflicted.* You jerked your head towards where the Amoebas nibbled biscuits and sipped hot drinks and said they were all so *evangelical* about their choice – so *smug.* You told me you liked the inner conflict on my face. You told me I had an endearing look, like a friendly goblin.

[laughter, noise of beer can opening]

A friendly goblin, Eva? It still makes me laugh. I passed you a cup of strawberry tea.

You said you were interested in people who fitted a certain profile, and I said you sounded like a serial killer.

You touched my arm and said we should go for a beer after the meeting, so you could explain your work more.

Lindy asked us all to return to our seats. It dragged on for another half hour. The tree was empty again – no doubt Morrow and MacBean were back in The Nova Scotia celebrating. But despite their successful prank, my original mission was on track – a drink with an attractive female. Revenge of sorts. As I listened to Michael tell us about his moment of asexual epiphany – in a basement darkroom, sweaty limbs grappling around him – I stared at the floorboards, the way the grain of the wood whorled into peaks and troughs, warped itself into faces and bodies.

Lindy thanked Michael and told us she'd see us same place same time next week. As the others got up to leave, Lindy handed me a clipboard and asked me to write down my contact details. I did as instructed and thanked her. She told me to come back, that they needed new people to survive. I mumbled that I would but couldn't return her gaze.

Outside, the sun fading, the rattle and scrape of bikes unlocked, goodbyes yelled as the Amoebas rolled off down the alleyway.

You jumped onto your bike and told me to follow you.

You sped off, standing on the pedals, arse raised in the air, upper body tilted forward. I fixed my eyes on your pert behind and followed.

You cut right onto Zeedijk and ploughed straight through the narrow gaps in a group of Japanese tourists struggling with shopping bags. They were still scattering as I followed through. You disappeared from sight for a few seconds as the street curved towards Damrak, but when I turned the corner you were still there, ten metres ahead of me. The lights changed to red as you reached the junction with the main road, and I pulled up next to you. My erection was back.

You looked over at me, unbroken eye contact, and just as I opened my mouth to say something, the lights changed to green, and you were off.

You cut down the Damrak and bumped up onto the pavement. I glided along in your slipstream, following every movement. You disappeared into an alleyway and I plunged after you, into piss-reeking darkness, a hotel ventilator blowing warm air in my face, pedalling faster, out suddenly onto Kalverstraat and across into another alleyway, and shooting out onto Nieuwezijds Voorburgwaal. A pretty impressive shortcut – I would have gone for the more conventional route. You crossed the tramlines into another alleyway and I thought I'd lost you, but when I came out the other side you were waiting for me.

In Cafe Van Zuylen, the beers came quickly, clunked down on the table, froth overspilling onto beermats. For the next hour, you talked about your PhD, your weirdo professor, enlightened Dutch attitudes to sex, and coping with the Amsterdam weather. I hardly got a word in.

You apologised for monopolising the conversation, gave me your card, and said you'd like to hear more about me. Could we get together again?

And so our meetings began. You had a knack for choosing unusual places. First it was a chess cafe on the other side of Leidesplein. Around us, white-haired men sipped *jenever* from thin-stemmed glasses and shifted pawns around while you whispered to me about Polynesian erotica. Next, a rundown restaurant in Chinatown where surly waitresses banged down plates and the air clamoured with guttural Cantonese and the hiss of frying. You wore a low-cut top and drank too much beer: you asked me how many people I'd slept with and I avoided the question by ordering more drink. The following week took us to a transvestite bar not far from the Amstel. In the blaring chaos of a karaoke session you slid your fingers into mine and asked me if I felt uncomfortable. I delayed my answer, breathless at feeling you so close, the soft bump of a breast pressing into my arm. I told you the surroundings were irrelevant.

On to our next spot, a bar in the heart of the red-light district, where we sat at an upstairs table – knees touching – and watched the traffic of punters, the doors opening and closing. You told me I should go to a prostitute for the experience, just pick one and go for it. I stared at the canal's surface and told you I wasn't interested. But the truth was that my sex drive was returning, and being at the heart of this sexual traffic both excited and scared me.

For a week I heard nothing from you, and began to worry that you'd abandoned me. But then, an email arrived in my inbox asking me to meet you at your apartment because you wanted to discuss something important.

You'd mentioned once in your offhand way that you didn't need to work for a living as your dad ran a mining company in Queensland and was pretty rich. Your apartment confirmed just how rich: a huge open plan penthouse on Keizersgracht, polished wooden floors, three leather sofas, a skylight window in the slanted ceiling. The living-room alone was the size of my place.

I spotted the kitchen at the far end, built neatly into a recess, a worktop the size of a kingsize surfboard. You strolled over and asked me if I wanted a beer.

I heard the fridge open, the clink of bottles.

I noticed a painting resembling a surreal mountain range, the peaks sketched out in purple and green against a yellow background. I stood in front of the mess of colours, trying to puzzle the picture out.

You pressed a cold beer into my hand and asked me if I liked the painting.

I said it was colourful, and you laughed. You said it was your hobby: painting orgasms.

We went to the adjoining room, which had more windows than walls. A blank canvas and easel was propped against the wall.

I sat on the sofa and you sat on the coffee table, facing me.

You said you wanted to talk about something awkward.

I shrugged.

You told me how lost I was. How I refused to talk about my emotional life, and how hurtful this was to you as a friend. You saw my potential but I shut out all possibility of meaningful human contact.

I picked at my beer label.

You asked me what happened, and I said I didn't want to talk about it.

You told me I needed therapy, and I told you I wasn't American.

You asked me why I was so emotionally constipated and I didn't answer for a bit, then I said one word: *Scotland.*

You said it was pathetic to blame my country for my emotional failings.

I took a mouthful of beer and said nothing.

You leaned forward to pick up your bottle, exposing the curve of one breast. You asked me if I wanted this intimate stalemate in my life to last forever.

I shifted uncomfortably in my seat – the beginnings of another erection.

I told you I had actually been thinking about sex again lately.

You said it was a sign that my subconscious self wanted to explore the idea of intimate relations, even if my conscious self didn't.

I looked at the soft place where your neck curved into your shoulder.

You locked eyes with me and said you could help me. If I was willing to talk about what happened – tell you my story, all the details – then you would organise sex therapy for me. In your opinion, this would go a long way towards fixing my issues.

I took a mouthful of beer and said nothing.

You told me to close my eyes. You told me to imagine a patch of wasteland in a city – a disused lot between two warehouses. Overgrown with thornbushes, tangled with weeds and rogue trees, all growing through decades of dumped rubble and rubbish. This was my emotional life, you said. Unkempt wasteland, strewn with junk. I would have to clear it, you said, if I was ever going to build again. You told me to imagine hacking through that undergrowth, ripping out the knobbly roots by hand, shovelling up spadefuls of crumbled masonry; until the plot of land was cleared, and there was once again a flattened space, ready for the foundations of something new to be laid. You can build again, you said. You can love again.

You got up and left the room.

A light-headedness overcame me. In the wall of black windows my reflection stared back. Beyond my ghost, Amsterdam glimmered.

You returned with a plastic bag. You said you appreciated that talking about my inner world to another human being was difficult for someone from my cultural background. You explained you wanted me to record my story on a Dictaphone. It would be less stressful.

I said I wasn't sure.

Tell the Dictaphone your story, you said. *Your sexual history, right from the beginning, every erotic encounter. All the background details. And what went wrong.*

And then what? I asked.

You smiled and said you'd design a course of therapy as we go.

I asked if it would involve shock therapy, and you said yes, in the sense that I would be confronting my issues. You said that the therapy itself would involve having sex. Different kinds of sex with different people. You knew people who could help.

I clutched my beer bottle tightly. It would've been easier to just say no, to walk out of your flat to The Nova Scotia for a pint, but the fizz in my blood told me differently.

I said we could give it a go.

You handed me the bag and said you'd send an email with full instructions. I peered down into the bag – batteries, a tumble of blank tapes, and the Dictaphone I'm currently spilling my guts into.

[tape ends]

Distillery Boys on Tour

I open the door to The Nova Scotia, and despite its shadowy gloom, clock Dingo right away. He's hard to miss: waving at me with both hands in the air, wearing plastic tits.

"Findlay McPhail! Yoo-hoo!"

Sitting next to him is Wee Stevie McKirdy, who parrots Dingo. "Yoo-hoo! Yoo-hoo!"

They collapse in a splutter of laughter.

My eyes adjust to the light. MacBean polishes glasses behind the bar and scowls in my direction. Apart from Dingo and McKirdy there are no customers in Amsterdam's only Scottish pub. I drop my laptop bag next to their table.

"Drinks?"

"Aye, twa pints," says McKirdy.

I go to the bar, making a mental note to keep my jacket zipped up to hide my bloodstained shirt. MacBean nods at me. "These clowns say they know you."

"Aye. My future brother-in-law and his pal. Esteemed employees of Cloudburn distillery."

"Fuckin numpties," says MacBean. "I'm seriously thinking about introducing a *No Scots* policy in this place. What you having?"

"Two pints of lager for the distillery boys, a pint of eighty for myself."

As MacBean pours I try to block out the cackling behind me. Wee Stevie McKirdy. He lived in Cloudburn's very own ghetto: a sprawl of council houses on the edge of town known as the Gully. All the houses had a weird brown roughcast that reminded me as a kid of chocolate krispies. McKirdy's house had an overgrown garden, car parts in the kitchen, and dogs and cats running wild. They were the sort of family that had a reputation for being unwashed – the five kids always seemed to have sleep-crust on their faces. Stevie himself was famous at school for crapping himself in P4 while the teacher read to us from 'Danny, Champion of the World'. The last time I saw him he was steaming drunk, running over parked cars on Main Street in Cloudburn, the tumble-thunk of his feet scampering over aluminium bodywork.

MacBean rings the beers through the till. Fizz climbs in the lagers, one pint fluffy-headed and one already flat. Looking at the beers, no doubt the first of dozens this weekend, a weariness assails me, all my troubles coagulating at once – Strange Fruit, the mess at work, the life I ran away from in Scotland – and I grip the edge of the bar until the anxiety fades. There's only one way to get through all this – by *keeping the heid.* I take the pints back over.

Dingo gives me a leery, beery smile and offers his hand.

We shake firmly. Dingo is drunk, cheeks flushed purple and his usually immaculate hair ruffled into a scarecrow mop. He wears cargo pants and a too-tight Italy football shirt. Up close the plastic tits are unrealistic, nipples like fat bullets. An aura of stale alcohol hangs around him.

"Hud a few beers already," he says. Dingo gulps at his pint and smacks his lips loudly. "As Winston Churchill wisely said, I've taken more out of alcohol than alcohol has taken out of me."

"True dat," says McKirdy.

I take a mouthful of my pint. "Where are the others?"

McKirdy answers. "Popped oot tae get some souvenirs."

Wee Stevie McKirdy is harmless, despite what a few car owners in Cloudburn might think. It's *the others* that worry me.

McKirdy nudges me. "Fin, ye have tae remind me this weekend. I need tae buy ma maw a fridge magnet. When I'm on the scoop I forget hings."

"I'll remember. So what have you been up to since you landed?"

McKirdy and Dingo exchange glances and smile.

"Been here most eh the time," McKirdy says. "But I popped oot tae get a 10p mix."

"What you on about?"

McKirdy smiles, eyes half-closed. "I went tae a heid shop. Asked the boay tae gie me a mix eh herbal highs n ony under the counter stuff he had." McKirdy moves his hand under the table and I hear the rattle of pills in a paper bag. "Just like a 10p mix fae Mitchell's."

Dingo butts in. "Except it cost sixty euros."

"How many of these sweeties have you eaten?"

"Lost count," says McKirdy.

"Orange yins are fuckin radio rental," goes Dingo.

"It's been years since I had a proper 10p mix," says McKirdy.

The 10p mix. A foundation block of the 1980s Scottish childhood, in the same gaudy tartan time capsule as school Burns' Day competitions, Halloween treacle scones, the Krankies and Wham Bars. It was a Saturday ritual, once I got my pocket money; or if we had no cash, Dingo and me would scavenge Cloudburn's undergrowth and roadsides for discarded Barr's bottles, prod clumps of grass with sticks until we felt the satisfying thunk of wood on glass; excavate the bottles from peat bogs, clean them in the burn, and take them to Mitchell's to cash in the deposit.

What a rush it was. Mr Mitchell behind the counter, walled in with sweetie jars, boxes of cigarettes, vodka bottles. The grand announcement: "A 10p Mix please, Mr Mitchell." The master of ceremonies sighing, reaching under the counter and taking out a massive stainless steel platter of penny sweeties. The challenge was to make your selection before Mitchell started swearing: usually around the one minute mark.

Dingo opens the brown paper bag and offers it to me. "Care to partake?"

I ponder it for a few seconds: perhaps a handful of random narcotics would calm my dread. More likely multiply it by ten. "Not now, Dingo. I'll stick to the beer."

I take another mouthful of eighty. The Nova Scotia. It's been long enough for the bittersweet taste of the beer to merge with the varnish and lard smell of the place and give me a delicious tingle of déjà vu. *Hullo darkness my auld friend.* I run my tongue along my teeth, enjoying the booze buzz prickling under my skin. "Ach, it's good to see some Cloudburn folk. Welcome to Amsterdam, gentlemen."

We clink pints. As I tip back the dregs I get a feeling of invincibility that's welcome right now. There might be somebody waiting for me at home. Someone who wants to return my Blackberry, and perhaps break my fingers. But if I've got the distillery boys with me I fancy my chances.

Buoyed with hope, I stand up. "This next one's on me as well. Same again?"

McKirdy attempts a thumbs-up and Dingo gives me a faraway grin.

Back at the bar again, MacBean racks up the glasses. "Ye still seeing that fox? What was her name? Eva?"

"Nope. It's finished, mate. Why do you think I'm back in the Nova Scotia listening to your shite?"

MacBean shrugs. "Sorry, Fin. She was something else. But it must have been great while it lasted."

I watch the eighty shilling swirl and settle, and think about the tapes I handed over to Eva, all my secrets now in her hands.

Erotic Encounter No.1: Angel's Breath

[noise of scratchy static, the microphone rubbing against something]

Right Eva, my sexual history. Where to begin?

Probably it's best to start by saying I'm uncomfortable with this whole thing. Emptying the contents of my head onto these tapes and handing them over to you. I hardly know you. But as you said, my emotional life is a patch of wasteland blah-de-blah, and to clear up the debris I need to confront the mess. You were right when you said that I need to try new things, even if it isn't your therapy. Live dangerously. So here we go. Headfirst into the void.

But before the juicy details, a disclaimer.

Point 1. As we discussed, the content of these tapes is confidential. You'll destroy the tapes once listened to.

Point 2. In return for providing these tapes, you, Eva Rosie of Keizersgracht, will organise sexual experiences for me that you think will expand my mind and help me overcome... how did you put it? My *current problems with intimacy*.

Enough. Here we go. My sexual history!

You told me to stick to the significant stuff, which means avoiding the usual gunk and splatter of a teenage boy's life. So I'm going to begin with my very own Big Bang.

[noise of beer can opening]

Sorry, I needed a wee bit of lubrication to loosen my tongue. This is tinny number five.

I started work at the Cloudburn Distillery a couple of days after finishing high school in July 1991. It was a summer job before university. My Da had got me the job – partly out of necessity, because my folks needed me to earn some cash before I went to Uni, but Da also wanted me to have an experience that kept me in touch with the working classes – although what working in the gift shop and the cafe had to do with the class struggle is anyone's guess. I didn't like the job much at first: I was one of those teenagers whose brain was still catching up with his body, gangly arms and legs, forever dropping coins and tripping over kerbs. So needless to say I kept making an arse of myself, the kind of behaviour that got me my nickname at school. McPhailure, they called me.

The job didn't involve much – mainly flogging various Cloudburn branded shite to Japanese and American tourists. T-shirts, golf tees, whisky miniatures, fleeces et-fucking-cetera. The most challenging thing was avoiding the creepy attentions of Morag Skelly. Morag was the gift shop manager, in her early forties and the mother of Cloudburn High School's infamous Skelly Twins – or the Tuna Twins as everyone called them on account of their fishy BO. She had curly red hair, buck teeth and big tits she always showcased in lowcut tops. On my first day she grabbed my arse – squeezed it, like I was a calf being assessed on the way to the abattoir – and I spent most of my time running around trying to avoid her.

After a couple of weeks they moved me over to work in the café kitchen. I was glad to get away from Morag. It was on one of these afternoons I met my future wife.

I was standing next to the dishwasher, inhaling its sauna-like heat, the stink of disinfectant and vegetables heavy in the air. A waitress clicked into the kitchen with a stack of plates. It was the burn on her arm I saw first – the sleeve of her blouse had ridden up to reveal blotches of pink and red skin, patches of flesh like melted plastic. In shock I looked at what the arm was connected to – a fiercely attractive teenage waitress in white blouse and black mini-skirt, dark hair tied up into a bun. She dumped her plates down on the stainless steel, wiped ketchup off her fingers on a paper towel, and rubbed the back of her hand over her forehead. Her nametag read KATHLEEN.

She scowled at me, and said *Want a picture?*

My reply still embarrasses me all these years later. *I'm Fin. I work in the shop.*

I work in the shop, she parroted back at me, turned around and marched back through to the café. I stood there, immobile, the dishwasher sloshing away in the background – guts churning, heart belting.

And so began my obsession with Kathleen Pinkerton.

A couple of weeks passed. I got moved back to the shop and only saw her in the staff canteen or once or twice crossing the car park on the way home. My heart ballooned and my balls shrank every time I saw her. I found out more about Kathleen from an unlikely source – Morag. Did I know the the new waitress, she asked me one day. *The girl with the burn on her arm? Black hair?* I played dumb. Morag told me that Kathleen's mother was originally from Cloudburn and had decided to come back because she missed the hills. Also because her marriage was over.

There were better places to start a new life surely but what mattered was that Kathleen was in my crap town and it felt like fate. After that first encounter my feelings had solidified into what felt like love. Every day at work was agony – waiting to bump into her and get the chance to finally say something meaningful. But I was a clumsy virgin and not really in Kathleen's league.

I finally got my chance one brilliantly sunny morning. The distillery manager Mr MacColl called me up to his office. Kathleen was already there. He told me to sit down and explained that the two regular tour guides were off sick and he needed us to rise to the occasion. There was a tour bus arriving in about forty minutes and we had to learn the notes and give the tour. He trusted our abilities, he told us, said this could be the start of something special. Then he gave us Cloudburn polo shirts to wear and showed us to the VIP Room, this plush blue-carpeted room where the tours ended and the tourists got a wee nip of Cloudburn, and left the two of us there on our own. We sat in silence for a few moments and then Kathleen spoke.

You work in the shop so you should know more than me about all this whisky stuff. She was glowering at me. I told her that was fine – I could lead the tour. As soon as the words were out my stomach flipped. I was shiteing myself. Up this close to her I could hardly breathe. She was engrossed in the notes and I couldn't stop staring at her: the burns on her arm, her hair, her bare neck. I felt like I was going to die.

We heard the revs of the bus coming up the driveway and something took over. Maybe that's the moment my career really started. My teenage clumsiness disappeared. I got up and Kathleen followed me to the reception. We saw their legs first as they got off the bus: shell-suit bottoms, tartan trews, tartan skirts, white bermuda shorts. American legs. They all piled into the reception and milled around for a bit, then settled in front of the distillery crest.

I still remember the first comment. One of the Yanks asked why the distillery buildings were covered in soot. I gave him my spiel. *It's not soot*, I told him. *It's a fungus known as Angel's Breath. It thrives on the alcohol vapour in the air. We are currently maturing around a hundred thousand casks on site so the fungus is having a real party. We repaint the buildings regularly but it's impossible to get rid of.*

They all murmured with what sounded like interest and I realised that I knew all this gubbins – I'd heard it from my dad since I was a kid. We took them through the distillery step by step, and they were gentle with us – maybe we reminded them of their grand-kids. Kathleen warmed up as the tour went on and even laughed at a couple of my jokes.

By the middle of August we were doing five or six tours a week together and miraculously, we were friends. I was comfortable around her but too shy to make a move. We would have lunch and take breaks together, sit out the back with cans of Irn-Bru, watch the buzzards on the hillside and chat about movies and music. We would sometimes go for a pint together after work.

I was pretty happy with the way things were going but time was moving quickly and before I knew it, August turned into September and we only had a couple of weeks left before heading off to uni. Every day after that was torture. Remember being a teenager, Eva? Remember being in love as a teenager? The memory's still sharp for me. I had to tell her I loved her: that was what it came down to. I couldn't just move away to a new life without letting her know. It didn't matter if she didn't reciprocate, I just wanted her to know.

So on the last day at work I was all fired up to tell her. Morning break, I'd decided. But Mr MacColl told me he wanted me to do a special job in the archives. This was disastrous news. The archives were stored in the furthermost warehouse building on the edge of Fairy Glen. It might sound stupid, but this part of the distillery spooked me out. Every kid in Cloudburn grows up on the stories about the Glen: an area of overgrown woodland where, legend had it, a clan of particularly evil fairies lived. Even on sunny days it's a dark and shadowy place and you can see why these stories sprung up.

So I followed MacColl across the courtyard, a bad feeling in my guts. He unlocked the heavy outer door and we descended into the basement. He switched the lights on to reveal a surprisingly large room full of boxes and shelving. The place stank of mildew. He told me to find anything I could on the Bottle of Brotherhood: there would be a bonus if I managed to salvage anything really interesting. I asked him why and he explained it was a request from the marketing department – he shrugged, as if it was all beyond his comprehension. He said he'd leave the door open for some fresh air. I listened to him leave and took a proper look at what lay before me.

It was clear that the Cloudburn whisky archives were in no way organised: from a quick glance through some boxes it seemed that the most recent stuff had been dumped near the door, so I headed towards the back of the room. It was unnaturally quiet, and every noise was magnified as I rummaged around through cobwebs and dust. Every time I turned my back to the door I imagined an evil fairy creeping towards me from the shadows.

After an hour of looking I'd found nothing other than empty bottles, accounts ledgers, and posters from old advertising campaigns. A mouse terrified me by scurrying between boxes and I was glad no-one was there to hear me squeal. I pondered going to the canteen for a break but was worried about MacColl seeing me. I sat on a box and felt sorry for myself. At that moment I noticed the book propping up a nearby shelf.

The Curse of Cloudburn, it was called. I pulled it out from under the metal leg and the shelves wobbled briefly before collapsing onto the floor with a satisfying crash. I was used to hiding myself in books and so I turned to page one, started reading and couldn't stop. It was crazy stuff – published in 1937, badly written, but addictive. The story of the Skene family, and how they had been cursed by the fairies for slashing and burning half of Fairy Glen to clear space for the distillery buildings. I was about a hundred pages in, reading about a gang of fairies dragging one of the Skene children into their underground tunnel, when someone came into the room, causing me to leap about six feet in the air.

Morag.

Isn't this cosy! she said, walking towards me. I could already smell her perfume overpowering the mildew. Sense the heat of another human coming towards me.

The place that time forgot, eh? She smiled and looked around the room. I had no idea where this was going. Common sense instructed me to get rid of her as soon as possible. But my brain was on the blink. Instead I stared at her, waiting for her to say something else, and before long my stare shifted to her cleavage.

She said: *You could do things here that nobody would ever find out about.*

She unbuttoned her blouse. I couldn't do anything except stand there, transfixed. The blouse dropped and she unclipped her bra. Her tits had white bikini triangles over the nipples.

You can kiss them if you want.

I rubbed a hand over one nipple, perhaps encouraged by this idea of the archives as a bin for the past. A place where I could conclude this virginity business and leave the memory behind in a mildewed box.

Morag unbuckled my belt and yanked down my trousers and boxers. I pulled my polo-shirt up over my head and as I did so her mouth closed around my tadger. I nearly passed out. My polo shirt hit the floor and she disengaged herself, wriggled her skirt up and sat back on a bed of boxes. She grabbed my wrist and pulled me towards her, pincering her legs around me, a queen spider trapping its prey. I was inside her before I knew what was happening, banging into her, each thrust knocking debris to the floor. And at that moment, just as I began to come, Morag splayed on 1973's ledgers, Kathleen appeared in the doorway with two cans of Irn-Bru.

I ducked. As if I could somehow be invisible on top of Morag, jeans twisted round my ankles. When I looked up again the doorway was empty.

Morag kissed me softly on the cheek. *It was nice. Any time you feel like doing that just ask.*

She smiled. The buck teeth again. And then she walked away, leaving me alone in the basement.

After a few minutes of staring into the distance, shag-shocked, trying to blank out the memory of the expression on Kathleen's face, I made an armchair out of some boxes and read *The Curse of Cloudburn* to the end. After finishing the book I raked around for a bit longer and found a box full of stuff related to the Bottle of Brotherhood and took it up to MacColl's office. He was pleased and gave me twenty quid cash in hand. I asked him if he'd seen Kathleen. He was his usual jaunty self. *Och, she was in a right hurry. Said she had a family event to go to, handed in her uniform and was gone by four thirty. Yill miss her, right ma friend?*

I said something about giving her a call.

It would be five long years before I saw her again.

[tape stops]

McPhailure

MacBean hands me my change. As I pick up the three fresh pints, the pub door opens: backlit from the street, two dark figures enter. Laughter and Scottish growl, and a bad feeling in my guts that reminds me of being thirteen. They roar in recognition when they see me.

"McPhailure!"

I ignore them and safely transfer the pints to the table, where Dingo and Gilly slump in a beatific daze. A hand squeezes my shoulder.

"Ye no talkin tae us, McPhailure?"

Douglas "Gilly" Gillies, the man who invented the nickname that haunted me all through high school, grins at me. His hair's gelled up into a punky mullet: a haircut that shouldn't be allowed on anyone older than twenty-four. Next to him, the gorilla bulk of Fraser Rae in a kilt with modern black leather sporran.

Gilly shakes my hand, then Rae.

"Gilly, Rae."

"Awbody calls me Razor these days," says Rae.

"Razor?"

Gilly sees the confusion on my face, and goes: "Show him why, Razor."

Razor Rae lifts his kilt to reveal his shaven genitals: long veiny cock, wrinkled balls, ace of spades tattoo on his pubis. I look away.

"We called him Cueballs for a while but it didnae catch on," says Gilly.

McKirdy goes: "I still think it's like, *totally* emasculating. Yir pubes are yir lion's mane."

Razor lets his kilt drop. "Ye keep yir face shaved so that lassies'll want tae kiss it, right? Why no yir baws n tadge?"

Dingo laughs.

Razor taps a finger on the table. "Since I started shavin I get mair action than ever. N one major difference – they always want tae teabag ma baws."

McKirdy shakes his head. "Are ye still thinkin eh getting yir tadge pierced? Whit dae they call it, a King Edward?"

Razor cuffs McKirdy on the head. "A Prince Albert, ye muppet. A King Edward's a tattie."

I'm still trying to blink away the image of Razor's genitals when I notice the tattoo on his calf. It's the modern Cloudburn distillery crest, the one I commissioned for the redesign two years ago. He sees me looking and puts his foot up on the chair so I can get a better look. "Aye, whit dae ye think?"

It's a good reproduction. I take a swig from my pint. "Nice."

"I want tae pimp it up a bit, ken," says Razor. "Gie it a death metal feel. Got an appointment for when wir back."

As Razor turns to the bar, I check out his head – bald as his balls. Changed days: in high school he was a heavy metal monster, hair down to his waist, constantly in trouble with the teachers for crimes against school uniform.

I was terrified of him back then. He was one of those kids who'd completed his journey through puberty by the age of twelve. A full head taller than anyone else in the year, with stubble, acne scars, hairy pits, and hobbies such as drinking, smoking, sniffing aerosols, sex, and fighting. The trailblazer in our year. Our paths had diverged during primary school but one day in S1 he passed me in the busy school corridor and lunged out to plant a concrete-knuckled punch on my upper arm, and before I even had time to squawk in pain he was gone, distant laughter swept away in the sea of teens.

After that, he developed a bully's professional interest in me. I was small for my age, and soft with puppy fat. He would dole out punches and kicks to me, Chinese burns and nipple twists, but never beatings – just the occasional whack, like the screw showing the prisoner who's boss. One day I found myself in an empty corridor, already late for my Religious Education class, when I pushed through the double doors onto the staircase. A pair of hands grabbed me by my pullover and whirled me round, tearing the v-neck. It was Fraser Rae of course: greasy hair, leprous pimples, AC/DC badge stitched on his jacket pocket. He rammed me onto the banister, scooped me up by the ankles, and dangled me off the side. Two floors up: far below, a crashmat of schoolbags. I hung there for maybe a minute. After all those months of terror, I just wanted it over with – if my teens were the supposed happiest days of my life, then I might as well just die now. But Rae hauled me back up and steadied me on my feet. He dusted me off, skelped me on the head, and walked away, lank hair bobbing as he went.

Rae left school at sixteen on a coopering apprenticeship with one of the big whisky companies near Alloa. I last met him a couple of years after school finished: I was on the shopping plaza in Cloudburn and saw him advancing towards me purposefully, a flurry of hair and leather and metal studs, fully expecting him to grab my nipple in his claw and twist, or just give me an old-fashioned kick in the balls. "Fin!" he said enthusiastically. He shook my hand, asked me what I was doing these days, wished me all the best for the future. His eyes were keen and genuinely warm and I realised he had no memory of bullying me. It totally threw me: the difference in character was so pronounced I could have been talking to a reprogrammed android.

I watch him as he opens his sporran to get his wallet. Fraser Razor Rae is still a big fucker. He has the sinewy build you would expect of someone who spends his days hammering and bending oak casks. He lifts his pint and drinks half of it in two gulps; pauses in reflection, then drinks the rest. As he picks up the other two pints and returns to the table it clicks that he bought himself two pints – one for the wait at the bar, and one to drink with the rest of us. Maybe I am still a bit scared of him.

McKirdy leans over and prods at Gilly's bag. "Whit did ye buy?"

Gilly empties the crinkled poly bag on the table. "Pack eh porno cards. Three magazines – Dutch Teeners 7, Pregnant Fuckers 3, Private 57. Two DVDs – Weapons of Ass Destruction, and the Scottish Loveknot."

McKirdy goes: "The Scottish Loveknot?"

"Aye, it's like this dead arty Braveheart-themed porno. Classy, ye ken? Sort eh thing ye could show yir lass."

Dingo shakes his head. "Pregnant Fuckers 3. You are one sick puppy, Gilly."

Gilly looks hurt and takes a drink from his pint. "Cmon min, they long winters in Cloudburn? It keeps me aff the streets. Anyway, who are ye tae say that pregnant women shouldnae enjoy sex?"

I butt in to change the topic of conversation. "How are things at the distillery?"

They all groan.

"Fucksake Fin," says McKirdy. "That's one eh wur rules this weekend. Nae work chat."

Gilly packs away his shopping and gets to his feet. "Howsabout a song?"

"Naw Gilly –"

"Sit doon ya fanny –"

He raises up his arms, Christ-like, and starts to sing.

"If ye hate the fuckin English clap yir hands!"

CLAP-CLAP-CLAP.

"If ye hate the fuckin English clap yir hands!"

CLAP-CLAP-CLAP. Gilly is the only one clapping.

"Hate the fuckin English, hate the fuckin English, hate the fuckin English clap yir hands..." He wobbles jazz hands in front of us.

MacBean shouts over. "This is a zero tolerance workplace, gentlemen. No racism."

The other distillery boys mutter curses at Gilly.

"The mother eh ma kids is English," says Razor, and for a moment I hope that Razor and Gilly are going to have a full-on fight in the middle of the pub, Godzilla versus T-Rex, and obliterate each other.

McKirdy rattles the 10p mix bag and this distracts them.

"Dinnae mind if I do," says Razor and picks an orange pill. He pops it into his mouth, crunches it and washes it back with a slug of lager. "Fuckin vitamin C tablets probably."

"Naw, min," says McKirdy. "I've been seein hings for the last hour. An apparition eh some posh cunt that I went to school wi."

They all piss themselves laughing. I look down into my pint and remember being fourteen: thighs black and blue from dead legs, the slow grey horror of Sundays.

Razor places a meaty hand on my arm. "Right, Fin. Whit's the plan for the night?"

"How about starting with some food?"

Dingo elects himself spokesman. "Sorry, Fin. But there's nae window for nutrition tonight. Entertainment only."

McKirdy grimaces. "Mind eh yon entertainment in Ibiza?"

Razor shakes his head. “That fuckin hotel should be closed doon.”

“Jugglers,” says McKirdy. “Different shite every night. Peruvian flute players. Some boy wi this eagle type burd swoopin around the bar. A fuckin magician. Parakeets on skateboards, min!”

A moment of silence. Then Gilly interrupts. “Seriously but, whit ye got planned for us?”

I take another swig from my pint and let them wait for my response. “I suppose we could go and see the district.”

Mutters of approval.

“But I need to go home first. Dump my laptop, get changed. Dingo can dump his bag too.”

Razor nods. “Aye, I could use a quick shower, get ma undercarriage fresh for later.”

“Right then,” says Gilly. “Let’s do it.” He tips his pint back and hauls a sports bag up from under the table. Silence as they glug down their beers in unison.

“Look forward to seeing you again, gents,” says MacBean as we move towards the door.

Out into fading afternoon light and street noise. They are loud around me, swearing and complaining, but the fresh air eventually quietens them – sobers them maybe. McKirdy nods over to where street-sweepers empty rubbish into a bin lorry. One of the workers is a female in her twenties, hair tied up in a ponytail. “Hot binlady,” says McKirdy.

The other distillery boys splutter and whoop.

McKirdy is shocked. “Cmon, I’m only sayin...”

Gilly hooks an arm round McKirdy's head. "Ye need tae sober up, wee man. Long night in front eh us."

McKirdy pushes him away, hurt look on his face.

Gilly lights a cigarette, cupping his hand over his lighter, and puffs smoke from the corner of his mouth. His clothes are as youthful as his haircut: jeans hanging off his arse, silver Nike trainers, a white Calvin Klein t-shirt and a shark-tooth necklace. The inked curls of a Celtic tattoo creep out from under his t-shirt sleeve like the squashed legs of a huge insect.

A hand touches my arm. Dingo. "I need a favour," he says, nudging me to the edge of the pavement. He rubs a hand through his mop of hair and glances in the direction of the canal. He looks at his feet, and finally, into my eyes. "Gilly needs a place tae stay. Yir maw said it would be fine for him tae crash at yours."

"What?"

Dingo chews his lip. His Italy top is speckled with dribbles of beer – dark wet spatters against azzurri blue, and even a few droplets on the plastic tits, like sweat. "Gilly booked his flight at the last minute. He couldnae get a hotel sorted in time."

My fists clench. I look over at Gilly, chatting and smoking with the others, shoulders bobbing at some private joke. "Dingo. This wasn't the plan."

"Cmon mate," says Dingo. "Or me n Gilly'll go find a hotel together."

I realise that if they do try to find a hotel, it means I'm going back home on my own. And the psycho-pimp is probably waiting for me.

"Okay, but any shite and he's out the fucking door."

Dingo smiles and slaps my shoulder. “Thanks mate.”

We turn back to the smokers.

“So whit’s the plan?” says Gilly, balancing a pair of sleek sunglasses on the top of his head.

“Fin’s cool,” says Dingo.

“Aww cheers, min!” Gilly does a thumbs-up.

Rae and McKirdy consult a map and point in the direction of the red-light district. I glance onto the canal and think about what to do this evening now there is an unexpected extra body in my apartment.

“Right,” says Dingo. “Can we go dump oor bags?”

“Sounds like a plan,” says Gilly. “Where d’ye live, mate?”

“It’s about a ten minute walk.”

Dingo gestures towards Rae and McKirdy. “The lads already checked intae their place,” he says. “Whit is it, the Sunnyside Hotel?”

Rae readjusts his kilt at the waist. “Aye. Think we’ll get the t-shirts oan then find a bar. Text youse later, right?”

“Can ye recommend ony coffeeshops?” McKirdy, looking at me through half-closed eyes.

“They’re all much the same.” The few coffeeshops I’ve been in have all been filled with ethnic cushions, coloured glass tables, and a dreadlocked, tie-dyed clientele lost in whirls of smoke and ambient music.

“Whit about the hookers? Are they aw much the same too?” Gilly howls like a coyote, drowning out the others’ laughter. I turn away, fumbling in my pocket for my bike key, a metallic nausea at the back of my throat that reminds me of licking batteries when I was a strange wee kid.

We watch Razor and McKirdy cross the bridge over Prinsengracht. Razor's kilt turns a few heads.

"This way." I lead the other two into a sidestreet. A clatter behind me, and I peer back to see that Dingo has taken off the plastic tits and dropped them on the ground. The cast-off breasts lie in the street like the central motif in a surrealist painting until a startled cyclist rides over them, snapping them into two separate tits.

"We had oor first beer at 10am," says Dingo. "How many pints is that now, Gilly?"

I watch the pair of them, noticing now the first signs of drunkenness – the occasional stumble, the wobbly heads.

Gilly screws up his eyes in concentration. "Six or seven?"

Dingo frowns for a moment as if to confirm a memory. "Aye. Seven."

"Seven pints," confirms Gilly. "Although the two beers on the plane wurnae pints. Just wee cans."

Dingo nods, doing the maths. "So it's seven beers but six pints."

"Aye, n dinnae forget the 10p mix."

We are interrupted by a mobile ringtone: 'Sureshot', by the Beastie Boys. Dingo fumbles in his cargo pockets and eventually retrieves his handset.

I look over at Gilly, the way he watches his feet on the uneven road, occasionally glancing back over his shoulder for flying bikes. He's not a big guy; I am taller by a good five inches, but he has bulk. His presence has matured into something deeper and more complex, and he knows it: there is a swagger in his walk, the way he spits at the road as if marking his territory, the ferret eyes darting. He was one of the cool ones at school: good at football, successful with girls, held his drink, talked to older guys as if he was one of them, wore jeans and a white t-shirt just like Jimmy Dean.

Dingo is chatting chirpily to his mobile, doing his best to sound sober, and it dawns on me it must be Ailsa. On cue, he turns to me and holds out the phone. “Yir delightful sister wants a word.”

A deep breath – here goes. “Hi sis.”

“Hi Fin.” Her voice is quiet. “Is he behavin himself?”

“Aye, he’s had a couple of pints, but he’s respectable.”

“Is he wearin the plastic tits?”

“Not anymore.”

“Listen – can ye talk freely? Is he at a safe distance?”

I lag back a little, and let Dingo and Gilly walk on ahead. They don’t notice, too busy chuckling at a passing hippy in orange dungarees.

“OK. Shoot.”

Ailsa sighs. “Somethin’s up wi Dingo. Somethin serious.”

“In what way?”

“Couple eh nights ago I woke up at 3am n he wasnae in bed. Found him downstairs in front eh the computer.”

“And...?”

“Google Maps.”

I'm silent – no idea where this is going.

She continues. "He was scrollin across Europe. Like he was plannin somethin. Runnin away, maybe."

"Ailsa, cmon. That's a big assumption. Maybe he was just... I dunno, swotting up for the pub quiz."

"He's actin aw weird lately. Did Mum tell ye about him writin poetry?"

"Dingo? Writing his own poetry?"

She laughs. "Aye. He went tae Alloa last week n did a readin at some sort eh spoken word event."

"What's this poetry like?"

"He'll no show me it. Says it's work in progress. This is why I'm worried, Fin. He's distant. Gaun through changes."

"He's probably just stressed, Ailsa."

"It's me that's got most eh the stress, worryin about our weirdo family."

"I remember the run-up to my wedding. Majorly stressed."

"Aye, n look how that turned out."

I puff down the phone in disbelief.

"Sorry," she says. "I apologise. That was well out eh order. Forgive me?"

I pause for a moment, letting her sweat. "Sure. You're my favourite sister."

I can hear her smile.

"But yill look after him this weekend? Promise me?"

"Promise."

"Call me, OK?"

"Will do, but I lost my moby."

"I'm aware of that," she says. "This Dutch guy called me half an hour ago. Ye programmed me intae yir contacts as 'Sister Ailsa'? Like I'm a nun?"

The familiar flutter of dread.

"He wanted tae know if ye were in this evenin. I telt him ye would most likely be out."

I'm shaking. "I better go, they've turned the wrong way. Chat soon."

I ring off and holler at Dingo to turn left. A bell trills behind me, and I step up onto the pavement. A twenty-something female bikes past, flashing thigh.

"Christ," says Gilly, shaking his head. "The lassies in this country are somethin else. Ye shagged many, Fin?"

I say nothing.

"What?" said Gilly. "None?"

"My private life is private."

"Ach," says Gilly. "Yir no short eh options here. Especially wi a salary like yours. Ye still spendin yir days makin up shite about fairies?"

"That's right. That's exactly how I spend my days."

"I'm sick eh aw these Yanks n Japs visitin Cloudburn," says Gilly. "Askin me where Fairy fuckin Glen is."

I nudge Gilly with the bony part of my elbow. "Maybe you could dress up as a fairy and stand on the ring road with a sign."

Gilly glowers. "Aye, ye think yir a comedian, ih?"

Dingo waves his arms in front of us. "Time out, girls. This is ma stag. Nae bickerin."

We cut onto Lindengracht in silence, Gilly whistling bursts of 'Scotland the Brave' through his teeth.

"Not far now," I tell them. I'm thinking: three against one. If the pimp comes alone, it's three against one.

"Dingo says ye get yir place for free," says Gilly.

I want to say no. "That's right."

"Nice. Awright for some."

Yir hands are dirty wi the blood eh the workin man, my dad informed me when I accepted the job – I am thinking about his bitter glare when Gilly speaks again.

"What was that wee lassie called ye were married tae?"

My grip on the handlebars tightens. "Kathleen."

"That's the religious one, ih?" asks Gilly. His mock-serious face betrays a glimmer of a smile.

"Correct."

"Did Dingo tell ye she's pregnant?"

I almost trip over the bike.

Gilly hee-haws, and Dingo immediately shuffles over next to me, up close.

"Fucksake Gilly! I was gaunny tell ye, Fin. Just heard last week."

We turn the corner onto Noordermarkt, a few kids messing around with a basketball on the cobbles. I try to focus on counting the bounces of the ball. *One-two-three-four-fi…* pregnant.

Pregnant.

"Never mind, Fin. A lucky escape," says Gilly as he flips his sunglasses off his head and onto the bridge of his nose, a fighter pilot zooming in for the kill.

Erotic Encounter No.2: The Gang Bang Gang

[Noise of beer can opening]

Hi Eva. I'm glad you found the first tape – how did you put it? *Professionally stimulating*. I still have my doubts about this but after making the last recording I felt lighter, unburdened somehow.

Erotic encounter number two is a difficult one to talk about though. It's something I've tried my hardest to forget.

It happened the week after I lost my virginity to Morag and the week before I left for uni. Late September. We had a bit of an Indian summer and adulthood smelled of freshly cut grass. After finishing work at the distillery I'd spent a few days drinking with old school friends, a welcome distraction after the shock and embarrassment of popping my cherry. I was worried about loads of stuff. We hadn't used a condom – was Morag pregnant? Or maybe I'd caught something from her that would erupt on my face in weeping sores. Or maybe, even worse, word would get out and Mum and Da would hear that I'd shagged Morag Skelly in the archives. Then I would walk through the town followed by whispers, walk through my own house facing downturned eyes. And on top of everything else was the agonising memory of Kathleen seeing me in action with Morag: leaving Cloudburn couldn't come fast enough.

One night in The Gothenburg a crowd of us were sitting at the corner table when Ewan Semple, son of the local haulage magnate, came over to the table to propose a *pre-university send-off party* on the Friday night. The Semple family lived in Girdlaw House – the mansion built by the original distillery owners. Ewan was desperate to be popular but in the manner of many rich kids in small towns, he struggled to make real friends. There was no shortage of hangers-on though: other teenagers milked his generosity, bled him for crates of beer or takeaway pizza and then ignored him when they got bored of his neediness. The party seemed like a good idea however – never mind the fact that only a handful of us were actually going to uni, it would be the last chance to have everyone in the same place together. We told him we'd be there.

I walked to the party around nine and already the music and shouts drifted down the driveway. A few teenagers – not from our school – sat on the wall outside the Semple house, swigging from bottles of high-strength cider. A Ford Escort with darkened-out windows was parked on the lawn. Numpties ran around the garden, whooping drunkenly. I walked round the side of the house to the patio, following the noise, and reached the epicentre of the party. Speakers belted out Guns n' Roses, sausages and burgers smoked on a rusty grill, cans of Tennent's lager floated in a bin full of watery ice. Everyone was already drunk and I had some catching up to do.

A couple of mates appeared and we stood there for a few minutes observing the action. It was at that point I noticed my sister Ailsa. She was standing at the barbecue, dressed grungily in a black blouse and frayed denim skirt, her peroxide hair offset by black eye shadow. The blouse revealed her cleavage and I noticed one of the guys she was with peer down her front. I knew she wouldn't have been let out the house like that – she'd probably changed into the Wonderbra in the bus shelter at the end of the road, or worse, in one of their cars. I wanted to go over there and launch my fist into the leering bastard's face. I wanted to grab her elbow and drag her away from these pervy older guys. But everything I said or did in Ailsa's presence those days was met with a nasal *fuck off!* and instead of going over I swigged more lager from the can, aluminium buckling under my grip.

A crowd of fourth year girls arrived and me and my mates decided to try our chances. I was still pining for Kathleen, but also in a weird sort of kamikaze mood. I looked back over in the direction of the barbecue and saw Ailsa tottering away on her heels into the shadows of the house and decided not to worry. Despite her recent rebelliousness, she was still a sensible girl. We pushed through the crowd to where the fourth year girls were clustered together.

It only took me about fifteen minutes to hook up with one of them – Lorna Pickering. Ailsa was constantly telling me that Lorna fancied me so it required minimum effort. She was a shy indie girl from Cumbria who hid herself behind curtains of black hair and long sweeping skirts but underneath the layers of protection she was a cutie. We chatted for a while about the new Sonic Youth album then peeled away from the others for a walk.

I'd read loads about Girdlaw House in my capacity as a tour guide at the distillery. There were all sorts of rumours about it being haunted etcetera so it added a bit of spice to our walk. It was neo-gothic, fake gargoyles and stuff, turrets on each corner of the house. Next to the main house was a big lawn and beyond that what looked like hedges. But when we got closer we could see it was in fact the remnants of a maze, one of those quirky Victorian follies. We joked around for a bit trying to lose each other and then we sneaked in behind the first hedge and started kissing. She tasted of sweet alcohol and ciggies.

Before long we were lying on the ground having a good rummage. Her skirt was so huge that it doubled up as a kind of blanket when I managed to unclip it. In the dark and with her hair down it was easy to imagine she was Kathleen. Judging by the way she clawed at me it wasn't her first time. I used a condom this time and it was fun – the smell of the hedge right close to us, and the wee noises she made like a baby being tickled. Afterwards I tried to help her with the skirt but I got the buttons all wrong and she got the giggles.

We walked back across the lawn towards the lights and noise. I was ecstatic – like I had cancelled out the Morag experience.

We got back to the house and pretended nothing had happened. I was drinking another lager when Ewan Semple stumbled into me. He was hammered, a big grin splashed across his face. I still remember his words: *Unreal man, there's an orgy going on in my room!*

It was a battle to get through the drinkers – first of all a ruck of people concentrated around the sliding doors, then a smoke haze in the snogging gallery of the living-room – couples draped on sofas and splayed on the carpet – and on into the hallway, where the sand-coloured carpet had been debased by a red wine spew. I heard a door slam further down the corridor and then suddenly there were more bodies in the hallway, five maybe six dark shapes moving towards the front of the house. I'd later find out the fuckers had dubbed themselves the Gang Bang Gang.

I squeezed through and reached a door with a Pearl Jam poster blu-tacked on it.

[A pause of several seconds,
something dropping on the floor]

Ailsa lay on the single bed, naked from the waist down, her blouse torn open and her bra twisted to one side. She was sobbing, or laughing – I wasn't sure which at first. I picked up her skirt and placed it over her lower half – and I felt a jolt of shock, a realisation of how bad this really was.

[pause for a few seconds – silence]

I found her knickers by the side of the bed and guided her feet through the holes. Then I helped her up and pulled the skirt round her waist and zipped it closed. She tugged her blouse back into place and I buttoned it for her.

She asked me what happened.

I looked around the room, taking in the empty bottles, the CD cases trampled into the carpet, shards of jagged plastic. I told her I would take her home. I was raging inside, wanting to find the figures I saw leaving the room. But the tightness in my throat told me to get her somewhere safe.

I helped her wash her face in the en suite bathroom. At one point she winced and placed a hand against her lower abdomen. We limped together across the room to the door. I popped my head out and saw the corridor was empty, so step-by-step we walked the hall carpet to the front door. There were still a few nutters jumping around in the front garden, so engrossed in their own drunkenness they paid us no attention. We walked down the driveway and out onto the main road, the music still belting behind us. It was dark but the lucid blue dark of the Scottish summer, not the kind of dark that's easy to hide in. As we walked Ailsa cried and she turned to me, face covered with tears and snot.

Don't tell, she said.

Don't tell.

[Muttering, noise of beer can opening. Tape ends]

Red Lights through the Night

I'm pulling on a fresh pair of jeans, the air in my bedroom thick with deodorant spray, when the buzzer goes. The psycho-pimp? I clatter through to the spare room, open the window, and look down onto the street.

A red moped is parked on the pavement, its tail hanging out into the narrow street, and next to it, the Thai delivery boy. He checks his watch, the door opens and he hands over the food. I hear Dingo speak – *aye thanks mate aw the best ih* – and the door closes.

In the living-room, the empty beer bottles pile up on the floor. Like me, Dingo and Gilly are wearing the designated stag t-shirts showing a crude design of a skeleton holding a beermug and a spliff, DISTILLERY BOYS ON TOUR emblazoned across the back.

Gilly unpacks the takeaway, opens up the aluminium trays and pokes at the food suspiciously. "Never had Thai before."

We huddle over the table and take turns to fill our plates with rice and curry and veg. Gilly crunches on prawn cracker after prawn cracker, showering crumbs onto the table.

Dingo speaks with his mouth full. "Fuggin good scwan."

It's dark by the time we leave the house. Despite the heavy clouds overhead and a chill in the breeze, Dingo and Gilly aren't wearing jackets, just their Distillery Boys t-shirts. My Dutch colleagues joke about this habit of British men, as if by acknowledging cold we admit some form of weakness. Hands in pockets, Dingo and Gilly walk with the swagger of the British lad abroad, heads bobbing with each step like malevolent chickens.

As we walk past the Noorderkerk, its sixteenth-century brickwork vivid in the streetlight, Gilly's mobile blee-bleeps. He flips it open and reads as he walks. "Rae n McKirdy are in Hill Street Blues, right next tae the red-light district."

The wind picks up and I zip up my leather jacket, hiding my own Distillery Boys t-shirt, glad to be getting away from the house. I glance back towards Lindenstraat and see a black BMW slowing at the end of the narrow street. Someone coming to look for me, or just a friend of a neighbour?

"Feelin pished now," says Dingo.

I glance over at him. Lazy eye drooping, he chews gum manically. His cargo pants are too baggy, and as he walks, the bunched material around his shins makes a rippling noise like a furling sail. His nipples jut into his t-shirt, and by the way his hands are wriggled deep into his pockets I can tell he's freezing. At this rate he might end up going to a prostitute just to warm up. *Wear a jacket!* my inner voice screams. *You're allowed to be cold, you fucking balloon!*

We walk quickly, and it takes us fifteen minutes to reach the top of Damrak. At the junction in front of

Centraal Station the main road, tramlines, cycle paths and pedestrian crossings converge on the same scarred patch of tarmac, and at this time of the evening on a Friday, it's pure chaos. Bicycle bells tinkle, car horns honk, trams clang, tourists laugh and shout and swear. Crowds flow back, forwards and sideways into each other, blending into one mass then separating again through the other side in loose formation. Cyclists whizz through the ruck, weaving around scattering drunks. Every time I pass through this junction I expect to hear the crunch of steel on bone, but somehow the pandemonium remains benign: an anarchic ecosystem that's found its place in an ordered universe.

We walk down Damrak in the direction of Dam Square. The greasy pavements are spotted with hardened chewing gum; Styrofoam junk food containers kick around our feet, pigeons hack at dropped chips. The air around us bristles with London and Scouse and Ulster and Glaswegian and Mancunian accents, stags and hens screeching and hollering. If I was a dog, would I smell the pheromones? When we're about halfway down, I yell for the distillery boys to halt and gesture over the road. We gaze at the row of converted warehouse buildings marking the perimeter of the red-light district, the canal reflecting the blaze of lights. Ahead of us, across a faded zebra crossing and along a narrow street, is the promised land.

Six hundred years: that's how long the red-light district's been here, in one form or another. It might not last another hundred if recent developments are anything to go by. The mayor, Job Cohen, is determined to clean up Amsterdam's image, and a third of the windows have closed in the last year. Despite this clean-up programme, my feeling is that the district will endure. If a multitude of sin has persisted in this warren of streets for six hundred years, surviving countless wars, empires, religious reformations, moral panics and technological revolutions, then surely an uppity mayor will make little difference.

When I first moved here I was surprised at how small the district is. The tales spun by British weekenders made me imagine the city as one sprawling metropolis of filth and sleaze. Instead, it's contained within a compact grid of alleyways spread across three canals, with only the occasional window dotted elsewhere around the city. My Dutch colleague Willem has his own theory. "It's a clever ploy by the Amsterdammers to quarantine all the asshole tourists in one place. It means we make lots of money from you and get to keep the real city for ourselves." A bike ride through the Jordaan on any Saturday afternoon confirms his theory – the fairytale streets and alleys are largely empty of tourists, and the cute bruin cafes are untroubled by loud British drunks, who instead are all crammed into seedy bars in the district, getting their wallets stolen.

Appropriately enough, in the fourteenth century the district featured many distilleries as well as brothels, so I suppose it's kind of a spiritual home for us Cloudburn lads. I lead us over the zebra crossing and Dingo and Gilly follow. A walk along this narrow street is like edging under the surface into a new world, a gradual immersion to prepare the body and brain for the excesses that lie further ahead. We pass a sex shop and a couple of raucous bars: ahead of us is a porn cinema. Without looking behind I know the boys are dizzily contemplating this sensory overload, bumping into other tourists. But I press on, determined to distract them with alcohol and drugs.

Hill Street Blues is packed. We step into blaring music and spot Razor and McKirdy instantly, the pair of them sitting at a table tight against the wall, several empty pint glasses stacked up. Razor grins, puckering the glass scar on his cheek, and waves us over. In front of them on the table is the *Gouden Gids* – the Dutch Yellow Pages – open at the escort section. Thai massage, gay massage, good old-fashioned heterosexual prostitutes, some with thumbnail pictures. Razor and McKirdy point at their favourites and laugh.

The pub is full of wasted tourists fresh off the plane. In the downstairs section a stag party in matching red t-shirts plays pool. Someone elbows me in the ribs. Dingo. "Fancy a pint?"

"Aye, cmon. I'll give you a hand."

We order five pints. The barmaid pours four and then the tap spits froth; she nods to the cellar and says she needs to change the barrel. I tell Dingo to take the beers over, I'll bring the last one myself. He nods and despite his intoxication manages to carry all four glasses at once. I pull up a barstool and fold my arms.

When you work in the alcohol industry, the first thing you do in a bar is check out the gantry. My vision traces across the rows of bottles, mentally noting the brands on offer, and I have to stop and doublecheck when I see a familiar bottle in the far corner. Cloudburn. It's half-full, and in this light hard to say how dusty it is, but it's in the same row as the other malts, the big sellers: Glenfiddich, Glenmorangie, Lagavulin, Jura, Talisker, Glenlivet. I gaze at the bottle, and in particular the labels I helped design three years ago. The front label is where I had the most input, and it's probably the single thing I'm proudest of in my working life. It's the same design Razor has tattooed on his calf muscle: a soft brown colour, like old parchment, the centrepiece a Celtic lion motif stencilled out in a striking graphite colour. Around the motif, the romance text flows neatly, almost symmetrically. Tiny gargoyle-faced fairies double as full stops. I'm reminded of Newt and laugh. The idiot. What does he know about whisky?

Unfortunately I never had my way with the shoulder label. Even at this distance I can make out the details. Kidney-shaped, the shoulder label sits snugly on the bottle's shoulder like a fat smile. The background is the same parchment brown colour as the main label, and the diagram depicts the distillery in accurate, if romanticised detail: the main building, with the Ochil hills rising in the background, the thin strip of the burn tumbling down the hillside; the adjacent warehouse, *CLOUDBURN* stencilled onto the whitewashed brickwork in building-high letters; and at the side, just peeping above the trees, the archives where I lost my virginity to Morag.

'Baby Please Don't Go' finishes and after a two-second pause, 'Crosstown Traffic' rumbles on. Somebody drums on a table.

Eva talked to me once about how everyone is sexually unique, and why attempts to pigeonhole people are pointless. The sexual fingerprint, she called it, saying that everyone was warped and whorled in their own special way. I rub a hand over my chin, anxious. Is this the real me, the one who sleeps with strangers? Or is it somebody else: the me I used to be?

Kathleen pregnant. I still can't get my head round it.

"There you go, mate. Nineteen euros."

A frothy pint sits on the bar and the barmaid looks at me, waiting.

"Can I have five Cloudburn whiskies as well please."

"Five what?"

"Cloudburn whiskies."

The barmaid's face is blank.

I point to the gantry. "Cloudburn, bottom right..."

I remove a crumpled fifty euro note from my pocket and hand it over. She fills the shot glasses one by one. As she rings through the round, I glance back at the gantry, at the shoulder label and its tiny picture of the distillery, and imagine that in its tiny sepia-coloured warehouse, a miniature version of me is standing in the empty room, walled in by boxes, no idea of the calamity and confusion that awaits me in the new century.

Behind me, Gilly laughs and laughs until he crumples into a coughing fit, whooping and hacking, and I raise the pint to my lips and drink.

Erotic Encounter Nos. 3-11: Sheep Skulls & Seagulls

[background noise of a scooter passing, fades to silence]

Next instalment, aged eighteen to twenty-three, 1991 to 1996. I sat down last night and wrote a list of my erotic encounters during these years and settled on a number: eight. I then spent some time thinking about how to talk about this stage of my life. In the end I decided I couldn't do it the way you want. A description of every encounter, all the sordid facts. No. Partly it's because I find it too difficult to dredge up the details, but partly it's because many of those details have been conveniently forgotten. It's unnerving to think that my brain has destroyed unwanted memories with the efficiency of a corporate lawyer shredding incriminating documents.

Instead of the erotic encounters, I got thinking about other stuff.

Those early days at university. The hall of residence smell: bleach, cigarettes, vodka, bolognese, burnt toast. Bedsheets stiff from cheap soap powder. The squeak of feet on vinyl-floored corridors, music seeping out from the rows of rooms, doors decorated with posters and pictures of bands and scribbled-on scraps of paper. All those eighteen-year-olds longing for belonging. The shock of Edinburgh, a city that had only ever meant two things to me as a kid: castle and zoo. I walked all over the city in the first few weeks, as if I could absorb it by memorising its streets and buildings, make it mine. After what happened at Ewan Semple's party I was relieved to be away from Cloudburn, but I was still struggling with the awfulness of leaving Ailsa behind.

The sex I had in my first year at university was casual and always unplanned. Too much booze, garbled conversations, the blindness of lust taking over, the dislocation of waking in a strange room next to a stranger. Unlike my new friends I took little pleasure in these conquests. On my long walks I would stop at pubs and find a corner seat: sip my pint and observe it slowly depleting, its fizz fading, and lose myself in a spiral of thoughts about what happened to Ailsa, the unknown whereabouts of Kathleen, what happened to Ailsa, the unknown whereabouts of Kathleen...

Then came the summer and my return to Cloudburn. This was when Ailsa's secret came out, and my parents didn't speak to me for a couple of weeks. It was a difficult time. Work was a refuge. I was a fully fledged tour guide at the distillery, getting better and better at the job, happy to work late to avoid the atmosphere at home. I also met my first proper girlfriend: Carol McEwan, a year younger than me and a waitress in the café. Yes, a substitute for Kathleen. A hockey player, with the lithe and muscular legs to show for it, she was sweet but with a hellish temper on her. We used to go up the hillside after work and throw down a blanket and fuck on the heather. The first time I thought I'd given her a multiple orgasm but it turned out she was lying on a sheep skull and its horn was ramming her coccyx. She slapped me. A beautiful moment. But Carol was patient with me: she taught me what to do. It's an interesting progression in the male lifecycle when we move from zero understanding of female sexuality to a working knowledge. That moment when we realise that one-dimensional grunt and push is the equivalent of unskilled labour, and from now on we'd better start learning the trade or we'll be on minimum wage for the rest of our lives.

Carol and I split at the end of the summer after a couple of weeks of arguments. In the days after the break-up we got on far better than we ever had as boyfriend and girlfriend. We're still in touch. She qualified as a doctor and lives in Australia, sends me wee messages with smilies and emoticons. Lots of pictures on Facebook of her blond kids, golden retriever, and yellow beaches – like she's trying to obliterate memories of grey Cloudburn with blinding brightness.

The rest of my time at university is a blur. I got serious about studying, liked the discipline and the structure. Sex happened from time to time. I had a reputation among my classmates as being too serious, and sometimes they would tease me gently about needing to loosen up in order to find a girlfriend. I surprised them on a couple of occasions by showing up on campus hand-in-hand with exchange students. Always exchange students: a Greek, a French redhead, two Americans. It was partly to do with me being different from the typical Scottish male student – I didn't hang around in a gang of lads, play football, smoke dope, spend every waking hour trying to prove how non-studenty I was. Maybe it was also to do with the exchange students' temporary presence in the country: the opportunity for both parties to get involved for a couple of months without ever really getting involved.

Ailsa came to visit me regularly in Edinburgh. The counselling had helped and she was piecing her life back together again, working at the old folks' home during the day, studying in the evenings for a nursing qualification. I'd heard through the Cloudburn grapevine that the guys who raped her were a bunch of neds from Stirling.

But sometimes she'd have rough days. One time in Edinburgh we were in a cinema queue when some boozed-up teenagers came bombing along the street. One of them ran straight into Ailsa and the shock of the impact triggered a panic attack. I had to take her back to the flat and sit up with her most of the night. I dozed off in my chair and woke at dawn to find her staring out the window. Out on the street, seagulls hacked at black binbags outside the local pizzeria. It took me three attempts to break her trance.

But thankfully these moments were rare. She was getting better all the time. My flatmates were good to her when I was at classes: joking around, going on walks with her, taking her shopping or out for coffee. Small kindnesses that added up. By the time I graduated she appeared to be a typical nineteen-year-old: into music, clothes, pubs, smiling often. Behind closed doors I knew it was a different story, but it was something that she had reclaimed the public part of her life. I started work and stayed on in Edinburgh, and Ailsa continued to visit every two or three weeks. I tried to persuade her to move through to the city, share a flat with me. But this subject always made her nervous and I learned to stop asking.

What I really want to talk about is what came next. The moment that changed the course of my life.

[tape ends]

Powder-Blue Bikini

The pints in Hill Street Blues taste metallic, watered down, but we drink three each and another round of Cloudburn chasers. At the end of the third pint McKirdy rubs his hands together.

"Time for a fuckin toke lads," he says.

Since the smoking ban three months ago it's no longer legal to smoke joints and drink alcohol on the same premises. Smoking is permitted in coffeeshops provided there's no tobacco in the joints. From what I've heard, most coffeeshops ignore this law and likewise the authorities too. Amsterdam makes way too much money out of cannabis tourism to sacrifice this cash cow.

We are barely out into the rain when McKirdy yells for us to go to the coffeeshop directly opposite. We go in, order drinks and take a seat.

I take a mouthful of coffee and watch as McKirdy empties the pockets of his cargo pants onto the table, laying out a Scotrail ticket, a crumpled map, a Mars bar wrapper, a scrunched up tissue, rizlas, and a Chupa-Chup lolly. He frowns. Then, as he gropes around in his inside pocket, his eyes light up and he takes out a crooked joint, tiny filaments of tobacco protruding from the end.

He sparks his lighter and sucks on the joint, tip glowing firefly red. I look out the window onto the dark street. There's a dead seagull on the road, one half of its body squidged into the cobbles in a mulch of blood and feathers, the other half sticking upwards, broken wing half-heartedly reaching for the sky.

"Seagulls," says McKirdy, taking another draw on the joint. "Rats wi wings."

"That's pigeons," says Dingo.

McKirdy offers the joint across the table but I shake my head.

McKirdy goes: "Aye, I suppose yir right. Seagulls are mair like…" A stream of smoke ripples from his pouted lips. "Seagulls are mair like… I'm tryin tae think of somethin that's like a rat but bigger."

I close my eyes.

Razor shakes his head. "Whit a fanny."

Silence. Gilly rubs his nose with the back of his hand. "Man, ma sinuses are still burnin fae that fuckin coke."

Dingo tuts. "That's what ye get for buyin it off some dodgy boy in the street. Cement dust."

McKirdy slumps back against the cushion, surprisingly effeminate with his limp-wristed smoking style, and even more surprisingly, the others say nothing about it. He lifts the joint to his puckered lips, kisses the end, sucks, tries to swallow the obvious splutter, closes his eyes. His eyebrows are ginger-white, skin the colour of a fish's belly.

Music belting, smoke curling across the ceiling, we huddle close to the wall as the joint moves around the circle, and although I pass on the first two circuits, eventually I relent and take a hot, dry toke. Apparently McKirdy's something of an expert, yet this is his first time in Amsterdam.

"This city is ma mecca, ken?" He bows with outstretched arms, as if praying to Allah. "It's an important trip for me. I've only got two days tae try aw the stuff I've dreamed about for years."

"Why did you never come to Amsterdam before?" I ask him. "The flights are pretty cheap."

"Girlfriend wouldnae let me. That's over now so I'm a free man!" McKirdy does a rap handshake manouevre with Gilly – shake, grip, bump shoulders – and then skilfully sucks on the tiny roach, its final ember glowing, pinches it between finger and thumb, drops it on the floor, and releases a stream of smoke through his zombie lips.

"Ken whit ma favourite word is?" he says.

Silence.

He performs a flourish with both hands. "Emporium."

We all laugh. "Ya daft…"

McKirdy raises a finger. "Or mollusc. It's a close call."

I shrug. "You could set up an oyster shop and call it the Mollusc Emporium."

McKirdy laughs. "Moll-usc em-po-rium."

Gilly sticks an elbow in Dingo's side. "Hey Dingo neebs. Aw this talk eh words. Maybe ye could gie us some eh yir poetry."

Dingo's face colours. "Naw..."

"Cmon, min," Razor says. "Wur chillin oot. Whit could be better than hearin the groom giein us some words eh wisdom?"

Dingo's eyes are bloodshot. "Ma poetry is sort eh personal, ken?"

Razor reaches out with open hands. "Yir amongst friends. Whit could be mair personal than that? Are ye tellin us yill go tae fuckin Alloa n read yir poetry tae strangers, but no tae us?"

Uncertainty in Dingo's eyes, but a glimmer of courage too. He nods, snatches at his coffee and downs it in one. The others are silent. Dingo stands up. The Distillery Boys applaud. Dingo clears his throat.

"This yin's called *Vinegar and Binbags*."

McKirdy has a look of genuine excitement on his face.

Dingo opens his mouth to speak – but it's a false start. He rubs a hand over his face, mutters to himself, snorts back a deep breath, puts his hands in his pockets then takes them out again. And then, in a sonorous voice, he begins his recital:

"While yomping through Fairy Glen, I got stung by a rain-drenched nettle..."

Silence, and I realise the whole coffeeshop is listening.

"Gazpacho teeth raked across my fingers, and it put me in mind of the sting of love..."

Dingo's face is rigid, cheeks purple, staring ahead into the unknown. Gilly is already doubled over. Razor has his fist in his mouth, and even McKirdy, gentle Wee Stevie, is ready to explode, eyes darting madly and face set to burst – but Dingo continues, staring at the opposite wall.

"But I remembered too, the missing flower..."

Razor is the first to go off: a string of snot discharges down his nose and he follows it up with a massive guffaw. Tears roll down Gilly's face. McKirdy is the last domino to fall, and covers his face with both hands, convulsing. Some of the other smokers in the coffeeshop glance over, amused.

Dingo stands still, mouth open. I want him to keep going, over-ride the assault, persevere. But he mouths a couple more inaudible words, flounders and sits down.

Razor coughs out the words. "The biggest pile eh shite..."

"You, my friend," says Gilly, "are the king of the bawbags."

McKirdy just sits there weeping.

I can't take my eyes off Dingo. He has the look of a man whose house has just burnt down.

McKirdy rubs the tears off his face and dangles his rizlas. "Another joint?"

Gilly smiles at me. "Fuck the ganja. Tell us about the hoors, Fin. Whit would ye recommend?"

"Naw," says Razor. "Porn. Tell us about the porn."

They're like pilgrims: the Three Unwise Men of Cloudburn.

Dingo elbows me in the ribs. "Cmon min, tell us everythin." He clearly wants to forget what just happened.

I sip my coffee and decide to give them my spiel. Part of me will always be that bullshitting Cloudburn distillery tour guide.

"The city has been tolerant of prostitution for hundreds of years. As a result, what's developed is a warren of backstreets catering for every sexuality in existence. Whatever you're into, you can find it in Amsterdam. Anything and everything. Maybe not in the red-light district itself, but in the city – definitely."

"Moldovan dwarves?" says Razor. The others laugh.

"Possibly, if you know where to look. The trick is knowing. There are really two sex scenes in the city – the public and the private. The public one is what you're about to see – the girls in the windows, the sex shops, the peepshows, the sex shows – the cheeky tourist experience. Stags, hens, ugly blokes, dirty old men. It's a service industry, and the city rakes it in. So you have to be aware that this is a tourist experience, a bit like a pervy Disneyland. You won't see the private scene this weekend. Sex clubs, fetish events, hardcore gay stuff, orgies. Behind closed doors, away from the district mostly. Stuff that happens in every city, but has added spice here. Because people move to this city for sex. People who take sex seriously."

McKirdy passes me a fresh joint, the size of a pencil, and I take a few draws, puff-puff-puff, let the smoke sit heavy in my lungs for a moment and then unravel out my nostrils. The stress inside me is uncurling. My life is fucked, but I need to let off some steam before I can see things clearly. They all stare at me, waiting for the rest of the spiel, and I pass the joint to Razor.

"My recommendation is look but don't touch. The red-light district is geared up to rip off tourists. I've heard stories about pimps coming through adjoining doors, nicking punters' wallets, knocking them around. Plus there's rumours of an epidemic of pubic lice right now."

They all look at me, and I keep my face deadly serious, hoping that my bullshit has put them off. As they nod and mutter the memory of my fight with Zasha creeps into my head. Blood on the carpet and screams from the other rooms. The knowledge that someone out there wants to hurt me does not mix well with marijuana.

The joint is now with Dingo, who smokes it with his hand cupped over his face and eyes narrowed mournfully. The joint goes round the circle another two times, and a silence falls. Gilly tips back his cola and gestures towards the door. "Let's go look at the hookers."

We finish our drinks and Gilly leads the way. I wait for the others to go first, and follow Dingo, my vision square on the back of his head as we squeeze our way through the smoky crowd towards the front door. I feel stoned, a little drunk. Cold air is what I need: cold air and a walk. Dingo holds the door for me and I step out into the drizzly street.

None of them – Dingo, the Three Unwise Men – have jackets. Gilly peers up at the black skies, rain already dotting his t-shirt.

"We can do a quick lap then dry out in a bar. Cmon." I start walking down the street, striding along the pavement, and look over my shoulder to check they've fallen into step behind.

I lead them down the Warmoesstraat past the sex shops and bars until I reach the turn off, and wait for them to catch up. They are wide-eyed, smiling, muttering and laughing. The street is busy: a crowd of lads in red and green rugby shirts walk along in a loose scrum, Yorkshire voices hooting, drawing a sneer from Gilly; a Dutchman in a rain-streaked trench-coat bikes through the drunken masses ringing his bell, and almost clatters into Razor; a scooter nudges along, one Moroccan teenager driving and one pillion, engine growling, eager to go full throttle; two police on mountain bikes glide out of an alley, heads flicking from side to side, looking for trouble. The street is sheened with North Sea rain, buildings and cobbles slick with it; I zip my jacket up to the neck, the damp already creeping into my blood. I look up towards the sky and see the misty drizzle illuminated in streetlight, cold droplets fizzing endlessly. I know this type of rain well and it usually sticks around for days.

"This way." Down a piss-reeking alleyway towards Sexyland, and when we turn the corner again, we are presented with a row of windows.

"Holy fuck," says Gilly.

The first window is lit overhead by a white striplight, and behind the glass door a woman stands glowering at the passers-by. Leather bikini, hair scraped up in a matronly bun, lips daubed harlot-scarlet. On the wall next to her a selection of dildoes mounted on hooks, like ceremonial swords: various colours and sizes, bulbous, heavily veined. She beckons towards us with a curl of her forefinger.

"Fuckin hell."

I'm not sure which of the Distillery Boys said this, but the sentiments are clearly shared by all.

Dingo speaks. "Whit's Sexyland?"

"Peepshows. DVD cabins. That sort of stuff."

They all turn to look at Sexyland. The neon glows bright in the rain: LIVE FUCKING, it promises.

"Could be a nice wee warm-up for the main event," says Gilly. "Cmon."

As we step through the entrance I think about Gilly's words – *the main event* – and decide that Sexyland might indeed be a good idea if the main event is what I think it is: getting Dingo through one of the striplit doors and into the arms of a prostitute.

I've been to Sexyland before, during my early days in Amsterdam. Working long hours, cut adrift in a new country and afraid of my lonely flat, sometimes after work I would walk around the city, taking comfort from the lights and crowds of people. Increasingly my walks diverted towards the district, and as I got bolder, into the sex shops. I was still struggling to get over all the crazy stuff I'd run away from; my interest in sex had faded. My visits to the district were an experiment in discovering what sexual feeling still remained.

Not much, was my conclusion. I visited most of the shops, and worked the racks like a professional pervert, never flinching from the images on magazines or DVD covers – double-dildo lesbian action, barely legal teenage girls, gay gang-bangs, cum lovers, shit lovers, piss lovers, old fuckers, pregnant fuckers, dogs, horses, pigs. A smorgasbord of gnarled veiny cocks and lube-smeared holes, fake smiles and empty eyes. I felt next to nothing: only a vague puzzlement that people could get addicted to this stuff. After these exploratory jaunts I would feel light-headed, relieved, and take great pleasure from a simple act, like making a cup of tea.

"So how does this work, Fin?"

Gilly points at the peepshow doors. This is the centrepiece at Sexyland: a circle of private cabins looking onto a revolving stage.

"You need a two euro coin."

A quick check round the group, and we all have the necessary shrapnel. Off we go into our individual cabins: doors slam and lock. I stand looking at the opaque screen, enjoying a moment of solitude. The coin in my hand can reveal the secret of what's through the window. It's an appealing concept – a Lion, Witch & the Wardrobe experience – through a door into a secret magic world. You never know what you're going to get, that's the problem. It could be a Slavic goddess gracefully performing an erotic ballet right in front of your window; equally, it could be a tubby couple living out their fantasy of shagging in front of others, and you get a hairy back to contemplate for sixty seconds.

My coin drops: the window clears.

At first it seems like the inner sanctum is empty: a crumpled silky red blanket cast off on the revolving platform, as if some princess has woken from a fifty-year sleep and fled the scene. But then I see to my right the girl's working the windows. Punky, spiked black hair, tattooes snaking up her body, she glides in front of me, splaying her pierced labia; eyes half-closed, she smiles in mock ecstasy. It looks like she might be amused more than anything. It's her nipples I can't take my eyes off – smeared with Vaseline and glitter, she looks like a mischievous sex pixie. A clunk, and the screen darkens again. Time up. I take another solitary moment to compose myself, and exit.

I'm the only one in the lobby – the others must have fed more coins into the slot. Dingo appears first, frowning. Next it's Wee Stevie McKirdy, then Razor and Gilly exit their doors almost simultaneously, laughing.

"Awww, min!"

"She'd teach me a thing or twa!"

"Oatch ya!"

"Just as well I've got a heavy sporran," says Razor.

The experience has sharpened their intoxication: the distillery boys hoot and clamour until Gilly peels away with a triumphant cry.

"Upstairs!"

We ride the escalator together onto the first floor. A row of DVD cabins. A bespectacled man with thinning hair roams the cabins with a bucket of soapy water and a sponge.

Wee Stevie McKirdy, wide-eyed, whispers: "The worst job in the world. Wankbooth cleaner."

Razor shrugs. "When in Rome, do as the Romans," and goes into the first cabin. Gilly goes into the next one, and Dingo the one after. McKirdy stands outside with me. We have the awkward air of strangers at a rural bus stop.

"Imagine the germs," says McKirdy. "Aw these pervy guys who probably dinnae wash their hands much, playin wi their tadgers in these wankbooths, touchin the door handles oan the way oot, gaun tae a bar n touchin chairs n tables, millions eh germs passin roond. Gonorrhea n syph n aw the other tadge-rot."

"Jesus, McKirdy..."

"I'm just sayin! I'm no touchin ony food while wir in these streets. Nae offence, but I'm shakin nae gadgie's hand either."

"Since when were you so picky about food hygiene?"

"I'm the health n safety officer at the distillery."

Silence. I sense that something is boiling inside McKirdy, and it turns out I'm right.

"Whit was that supposed tae mean? *Since when wir ye so picky about food hygiene?*"

He thinks I've implied he is unclean. The badge he's struggled to unpin all of his adult life.

"Stevie, I'm sorry. That wasn't what I meant."

He looks at me with defiance, chin jutting out. "I shower twice a day. Floss. Use a tongue-scraper.

Deodorant. Foot creams. Ma hoose is fuckin immaculate, min. But they still call me McStinky just cause I'm fae the Gully."

"And because you shat yourself in P4."

My quip was risky but he laughs.

"Aye, long memories you fuckers."

"Same with me," I offer. "You all still call me McPhailure. You all still think I'm a posh weirdo."

"True dat," says McKirdy.

Razor's door opens and he bundles out, straightening his kilt. "That's some seriously fucked up porn thuv got. Ye can scroll through aw sorts eh stuff. Pigs, min!"

Dingo emerges. His face is white. It's another couple of minutes before Gilly comes out, chuckling.

"I made sure the wankbooth cleaner would have tae work for his money," he says.

McKirdy shudders. "Ye didnae..."

"Aye," says Gilly. "Oan the screen."

They groan. Razor pats Gilly on the shoulder. "I cracked one off n aw, mate. Good tactics, ken – yill last longer wi the ladies."

As we go back downstairs and out into the night, my only consolation is that they've already depleted a chunk of their collective energy before we begin our tour of the windows. I glance over at Dingo, who stumbles as he walks – fading fast, by the look of things.

Outside Sexyland, I lead them past a few windows – a busty Latin woman wearing a pink teddy, a teenage blonde Dutch girl chewing gum and rocking her hips, a bored-looking woman with short afro chatting into her mobile phone – and then turn down an alleyway only a metre wide, windows on either side, warmer and drier than the street we just left behind. We walk in single file with me in the lead.

As we pass by, the girls tap on the glass and smile and pout, but I don't look, just keep my eyes fixed on the way ahead. Punters walk towards us from the opposite end of the alley and we squeeze past, shoulders brushing leather and Gore-Tex and polyester, a flow of men in both directions down this narrow valley in the ancient buildings, an underground stream of horny blokes. The exit beckons ahead and suddenly I'm aware that I can't hear the distillery boys behind me. I glance behind and see they've stopped at a window ten metres back – the door is open and the girl leans out into the alley, talking to them. I walk back, already nervous in my gut, because I think I know who they're chatting to.

Gilly is doing the talking, his voice low, confident. It's her. My hunch was right. The girl in the powder-blue bikini, the most beautiful girl I think I've ever seen. Last month, Eva organised an appointment with her as part of my ongoing therapy. Tall, curvy, sandy blonde hair, soft blue eyes and a flawless body. She told me her name when I gave her the money – Larisa, from Latvia – and she tugged the red curtain back across the door and told me to go into the bathroom, undress and wash myself.

When I re-emerged from the bathroom she was also naked, the powder-blue bikini neatly folded on a shelf next to a compact stereo, radio turned down low. She grinned and told me to lie down on the bed. Her pubic hair was trimmed in a neat blonde fuzz and crowned with a tiny tattoo of a butterfly.

I lay on the bed, she stroked my chest, worked her way down. Radio softly murmuring, the distant laughter of some punters outside. *Therapy*, I reminded myself.

She'd kissed my cheek as I left, the door closing shut behind me, and I rubbed my hand over my mouth, smelling the strawberry condom on my fingers.

Gilly leans in through the open door. "You're absolutely gorgeous, Larisa – I've never seen a lady as beautiful as you before."

She smiles shyly, well-rehearsed, and when she glances over at me, I see a flicker of recognition in her eyes. I look down, away, then at the others. Dingo stares at her in rapt concentration. Razor leers openly, tongue resting on his upper lip. Only McKirdy shows little interest, surreptitiously checking his mobile.

"How much for a blow job?" Gilly grins, now holding her hand.

"Fifty euros," she says. "I'm the best in the district."

"How about doing it for free? A handsome guy like me?" Gilly now holds her wrist. "You can't get many guys as handsome as me coming by."

She smiles sweetly, then with her other hand, shoves him in the chest, and he stumbles back, releasing her wrist. Smoothly and swiftly she shuts the door in our faces and locks it with a quick turn of the key. And she raises her middle finger, face suddenly emotionless. Gilly shrugs and laughs, turns away. "Frigid bitch," he says.

I walk quickly towards the alleyway exit. A quick glance behind shows they are following in step, Gilly and Razor sharing a joke, Dingo with his hands deep in his pockets, McKirdy still thumbing the keypad of his mobile. I step out of the alleyway onto the street again, into steady rain and a rising breeze.

The view before me is strangely beautiful. Raindrops shatter the surface of the canal, and the reflected buildings and lights ripple and shimmer in the water. On the opposite side of the street, almost every doorway has a neon sign above it, glowing reds and yellows and blues advertising sex shops, bars, coffeeshops, restaurants. The grand old buildings stand firm in the face of the rain, their seventeenth-century facades resolute, the red brickwork smudged with damp. In the upper levels of the townhouses, I see lights on, plants in the windows, paintings hanging on walls, mirrors, indistinct figures moving around IKEA-furnished rooms, people living normal lives a couple of levels above the whoring and the drugging. A ceiling is all that separates the two worlds.

When the boys fall into step next to me I start walking again. We pass a row of windows, at ground and first floor level, and the girls knock on the windows, sway their hips, bounce their tits, smile, wave. I keep moving, determined to drive onwards. "There's loads to see," I tell them. "We can do a lap then get a drink. There's plenty of time."

Gilly pats my shoulder as we walk. "Cheers for the tour, min. This place is a fuckin fantasyland."

I ignore him and step off the pavement towards one of the bridges crossing the canal. "Follow me."

For the next thirty minutes we tramp through the alleyways, through the shuffling crowds, the air misted with breath and drizzle. The same crowd of Yorkshire rugby players pass us once more, but this time Gilly is too busy leering in a window to see them. The girl stands motionless, staring back at him as he presses himself against the window and grinds his crotch into the glass. I'm the only one who notices: the others are a few metres away, pointing at a cluster of windows where an Asian girl readjusts her thong.

We stop at a snack bar and they buy slices of tandoori pizza – even McKirdy, who seems to have forgotten his pledge about food in the district – and I watch as they graze, crumbs of curried chicken falling at their feet, strands of cheese dangling over the edge of their cardboard holders, chins shining with grease. "Need a beer," mumbles Dingo.

By the time we complete the circuit I need a beer too. Rain drips off my nose as we return to the Oudekerk, and McKirdy yells through the rain. "This yin!" he shouts, and points at the Irish pub on his right.

Erotic Encounter No.12: Through the Bookshelves

The predictable beginning...

[noise of beer can opening]

I should've put the beer in the freezer though... fucking hot out there. Now, where was I?

Ah. The moment that changed the course of my life.

A washed-out day at the end of August 1996. The Edinburgh Festival was drawing to a close and the city had its usual air of exhaustion and relief. After a week of drinking and going to see comedy shows with my colleagues I wanted away from the chaos for the weekend. Some peace and quiet. As I was walking up Lothian Road I decided that a book would be a good way to lose myself until returning to work on Monday. So I took a diversion down the West Port, heading towards a second-hand bookshop I'd passed but never explored.

I opened the door and stepped into the dark shop and a smell of dusty books. The owner was sitting behind the till. He raised his eyes from his book, examined me with a suspicious stare, and returned to his reading. I crept through to the back of the shop to where a handwritten sign on crumpled cardboard advertised popular literature. Books were arranged neatly on the shelves in alphabetical order but at some point they'd run out of space and piled the books in leaning towers against the wall, as if insulating the shop from the Edinburgh weather. I decided to start with *A* and began browsing.

I stumbled across an anthology of erotic short stories and after checking the owner wasn't watching, had a peek inside. The bell pinged and someone came into the shop and I repositioned myself so that I could see anybody coming down the aisle towards me. A murmur of voices and the clump of footsteps towards the back of the shop and I carefully replaced the anthology and picked up the collected works of Dylan Thomas. The newcomer moved into the parallel aisle to me and from where I was crouching, I could see her denim-skirted legs between the shelves.

The legs moved, and then I saw a hand with red fingernails reach down to pick up a book. The hand was attached to an arm with pinkish blotches starting just above the wrist, blotches that seemed to have faded with time until they were almost the same colour as the skin – but not quite. I edged further along the aisle until I found another gap in the books, peered through, and saw her in profile.

Kathleen Pinkerton, framed in the light from the main window, wearing a long-collared white blouse with the denim skirt, bare sunbrowned legs and an old pair of sandals. A pocket umbrella dangling from a hook on the shoulder-bag. She was frowning, tilting her head to get a better look at the titles.

I stepped back and turned away from her to face the military history section. It had been a long time: five years. During that time I'd been to university, had my first relationships, completed my university degree, and tried my best to grow up. And here she was: my first ever love, just one bookshelf away.

My feet told me what to do. As I approached her she stepped back to let me past, but instead of passing I stood there, looking at her. She sensed the attention and looked up.

I said one word: *Hi.* Not the best of opening lines, but I wasn't sure what else to say.

Her frown intensified. A few seconds passed before she spoke. *Fin.* She laughed. *Do you still work in the shop?*

I opened my mouth to speak but nothing came out.

She readjusted the shoulder strap of her bag then gave me a smile. *You look older.*

I wasn't sure if this was a compliment or not. She asked me what I was doing these days and I said it was a long story. She asked if I fancied a pint. We went to the Blue Blazer, thankfully free of tourists. On the way we talked about Cloudburn – her mother still lived there but she didn't go back much, maybe once a year. As I ordered drinks I watched her in the bar mirror. She looked good, a bit softer and more feminine than I remembered. And she no longer drank pints of cider – she asked for vodka and ginger ale.

I asked her about the last five years.

She stirred her drink, removed the plastic swizzlestick, licked it, and deposited it in the ashtray. Her voice had a defensive edge. She'd gone to Aberdeen University, got a 2:1 in English, moved to London to work at a publishing house, travelled for six months, and now here she was, back in Scotland temping with an insurance firm.

I told her I'd been in Edinburgh since leaving Cloudburn five years previously. Got my degree in Marketing, worked my summers as a tour guide at the distillery – she looked surprised – and that I was continuing the link by working for MacKenzie & Grierson, the company that owned Cloudburn, as Customer Account Manager for Northern Europe, organising shipments of the company's various spirit brands.

I sipped my pint. She hooked her fingers into her drink, gouged out the ice, and dumped it into the ashtray next to the swizzlestick. I asked if she wanted to remove the ginger ale as well.

She laughed and said she was picky. Then her face changed, went all mysterious. *Tell me the gossip from the distillery*, she asked.

There wasn't much to tell. I'd gone back three summers in a row and by the end of the first I was the lead guide. I told Kathleen how I developed the Curse of Cloudburn tour, hoping she'd be impressed, told her the visitor numbers had increased twenty percent. She kept looking at me with this mysterious face, and I realised she was probing at the one subject I wanted to forget – that of Morag Skelly.

Occasionally Morag and I had passed each other in the canteen or the car park and she'd give me this wee smile. During the third summer she was off work because she needed an operation on her knee. A massive relief.

Then Kathleen came out and said it: *Are you still into older women?*

She knew how to twist the knife. I told her that Morag was an accident and I stood up and retreated to the bar to get more drinks. It was clear Kathleen never suspected I'd been in love with her.

When I got back to the table she could see how embarrassed I was and tried to change the subject by congratulating me on ordering her drink minus ice and swizzlestick. I asked her about her travels – *were you away discovering yourself?*

She must have heard the sneer in my voice because she was timid as she reminisced about backpacking through Asia and South America – last stop New York, then home. Her stories made me uncomfortable – to my embarrassment I'd never even been on a plane. Again, I was reminded of the distillery days, when she seemed light years away from me, unobtainable. *Some amazing experiences*, she told me, and I wondered if any of these experiences had been sexual.

I asked her where her favourite place was and she said that everywhere had its moments, but Melbourne was particularly special. *Made some friends. Met a guy.*

Ahh. There it was. I realised I'd been waiting for this moment and was surprised how disappointed I was.

I asked: *Australian guy?* As in, someone who lives on the other side of the world. Fingers crossed for a doomed relationship.

English, she said. *His name's Tyrone.*

Is. Present tense. I took a mouthful of eighty shilling and imagined a muscly black guy with a London accent, his hardman stare pointed in my direction.

She asked if there was any romance in my life.

Since I'd last seen her my apprenticeship in love and lust had been completed, but not with any distinction. I wasn't sure what to tell her. What should I have said, Eva? What would have impressed a twenty-three-year-old female with more life experience than me?

I sat staring into my pint, wondering how exactly to summarise my state of sexual being.

Well? said Kathleen. *Wife? Girlfriend? Nudge-nudge?*

I told her I was *mostly single*. I thought this had enough mystery to make me sound interesting but she hooted with laughter.

We swapped phone numbers when we left the pub and it became a regular thing. We'd meet every week or so, usually on a weeknight or a Sunday, and go for a few drinks or to see a movie. It was a strange time. I wasn't in love with her anymore, but kind of in awe of her instead. Friendship was a comfortable option. Besides, there was the invisible presence of Tyrone. He never visited Edinburgh, but Kathleen would disappear down to London to see him from time to time. She seemed happy with the arrangement. She never talked about him in detail but I got the impression that so long as she got her fix of love-slash-sex every six weeks or so then her batteries would be recharged and she could get on with the uncomplicated business of living her life.

And so the months passed. I did well at work and took on a couple of extra customers. The team leader told me he was impressed with my ability, attitude and knowledge, and I wasn't sure if I should be glad or not. The company seemed to have me earmarked to progress into middle management, but if the team leaders were my future, then the future was a scary place. There were five of them, all in their thirties or early forties, overworked and constantly regurgitating corporate mantras. On the other hand, staying in the job I was doing for more than another year was also a scary prospect. Many of my peers had worked in the office since leaving school and were now in their mid-twenties, yet still living with their parents, suspended in cryogenic adolescence. Others were faded forty-somethings or graduate drifters. I distanced myself from them all without being rude.

I had my eye on the department next door – Product Development and Marketing. They designed and redesigned the company's brands, marketed them, travelled around the globe. his was where I wanted to be within the next year or two.

Kathleen rarely talked about her temp work at Scottish Standard. It was clear the job depressed her, but she showed little inclination to look for anything else. On our nights out she rarely talked about personal stuff and instead we stuck to safe subjects like music, movies, books, politics, work gossip. Our friendship gradually grew stronger but intimate would be the wrong word to use – safe was probably a better description. I think we were both just glad to have somebody to stop us from being alone.

It couldn't go on like that forever and things finally changed when she told me about the burns on her arms.

[slurping noise, muttering]

When I got reacquainted with Kathleen in Edinburgh that summer, the burns were less noticeable. Occasionally when she tied back her hair or looked at her watch I would catch a glimpse of the blotches and always found it hard to stop staring. I didn't ask her about what happened because I knew her personal life was off-limits. One year we'd hung out, more or less going on dates – movies, drinks, meals – and in all that time we had never come close to kissing or drunkenly going home together.

One night we decided to go for a curry and ended up in a Nepalese place close to Haymarket station. There was some kind of family reunion going on, a dozen people taking up one side of the restaurant. The noise they made gave us a weird kind of intimacy – everything we said was only audible to ourselves thanks to the party's drunken laughter. We'd just eaten a pakora starter and had ordered our second beers when I asked Kathleen if she was going to London soon to see Tyrone.

I remember the next part very clearly – she picked up a shred of lettuce from her plate and dabbed it onto the end of her tongue and chewed thoughtfully. Then she said: *There is no Tyrone.*

I was perplexed.

There never was a Tyrone.

Our tikka masala and rogan josh arrived. Kathleen began to spoon rice onto her plate, face turning slowly purple. *I'm sorry I lied to you*, she said.

This, she said, rolling up her sleeve and revealing the burns, *This is why I invented Tyrone.*

Two bottles of Cobra on the restaurant table, another gust of laughter from the family reunion crowd, the twang of sitar music. I didn't know what to say.

She told me the story. How, at the age of three, she had pulled a pot of boiling cock-a-leekie soup off the stove and it had tipped down one side of her body. Her earliest memory: the pain, and a steaming puddle of shredded leeks on the floor. Growing up a scared, tearful child, easily spooked by barking dogs, thunderstorms, motorbike engines, fireworks, loud music. Always conscious of the burns on the right side of her body, as if people could see through her clothes.

Like everyone in the world had x-ray vision, she said, tears running down her cheeks and under her chin. *Eat*, she told me, and I half-heartedly took a few mouthfuls of rogan josh.

Things changed when she was twelve and discovered long distance running. Free at last. She joined a harriers club and would go out three or four nights a week, a crowd of young runners in white t-shirts ghosting through various Glasgow suburbs, through parks and housing estates, and she loved that feeling of her feet striking the ground and her pony tail bouncing on her back, that feeling of running away from who you were, a freedom that she'd never experienced before. And from this she got a kind of bolshie confidence, and the world was no longer scary, and the burns were just part of who she was.

In her teenage years, the confidence came and went. At school, she was quite popular – she was sporty and bright, and pretty enough to get the right sort of attention and avoid the wrong sort. There was a setback when she was fifteen and wore a sleeveless dress to the school Christmas party, thinking that the beauty of the sparkly blue dress would outshine the burns on her arms, but no, a couple of the older girls – *absolute fucking bitches* – had been drinking cider in the car park and followed her round the dance floor, prodding the burns and asking if she had AIDS.

When her parents split up it all got a bit too much, which was around the time she moved to Cloudburn – *when I met you*, she said with an emphasis and sincerity that shocked me. But then she went to Aberdeen uni and overall it was a good time and she made lots of great friends – Kathleen now talking at a hundred miles an hour, clearly drunk, the family party putting their jackets on and glancing over – but she lost the confidence she'd found jogging those long miles and hid herself in a shell. *What's the word*, she asked me, *a carapace*? I told her that this was indeed the word. She had two boyfriends at Aberdeen but could never really get used to the whole taking her clothes off thing. And in London she'd dated no-one. Travelling? A one-night-stand in Sydney with a Welsh guy where she lost all inhibitions and had *an amazing time* – I flinched involuntarily – *but this was a difficult feeling to recapture, you know*? That lack of self-consciousness, that likelihood that when you take your kit off the other person is not going to be shocked by these burn marks.

She began to eat voraciously, scooping up the luridly red curry and talking at the same time, pausing to slug on her Cobra. Maybe that was the moment I fell in love with her again.

After paying the bill we walked back towards Bruntsfield and stopped for a couple more drinks. She was teary, angry, borderline violent, glowering around the pub looking for a challenge. In an effort to calm her I took her hand and held it. She squeezed my fingers tight, as if emptying her rage through her hand.

She asked me to walk her back.

It was only five minutes, and when we got to her door, she held it open for me. I followed her, up three flights of stairs and watched her rummage in her handbag for a full two minutes until she found her key. Her flatmates were out, so the place was quiet. She made us tea and seemed to have calmed down. We sat in her room.

She said she didn't know what to do. Her life was a mess. I told her she had a lot to offer and she laughed and asked me if I wanted to see them. I didn't know what she meant but then she started undressing and I realised she meant the burns.

I told her to stop but her blouse was off and she yanked her jeans down.

The burns were striking, a series of melted welts down her arm, and then spattered across one side of her body, from her ribcage down to her thigh.

She said: *See how it ruined my life?*

She sat down heavily on the bed next to me, face buried in her hands, sobbing. She started going on about how *it never got my face at least. I don't know why this is fucking me up so much but it is, I can't help it, it just is.*

I kissed her arm. I don't know where the idea came from, but that's what I did – I leaned across and kissed the burn, brushed my lips along the length of her arm and ended by kissing the side of her head near her ear. I told her I thought she was beautiful, and thought so from the moment I first saw her standing next to the dishwasher.

She started laughing through her tears and told me I was a fucking idiot. Did I know that? A fucking idiot.

I shrugged.

Then she said it was the nicest thing anyone had ever done to her. *Kiss me again*, she said.

I kissed her arm again, feeling the rough skin under my lips. It didn't feel weird, on the contrary, it was probably the sexiest thing I'd ever done in my life. I sought out every burn mark on her body – ribcage, waist, thigh – and kissed it. She draped her arms around me and held me close.

Stay the night, she said. And I did. For eight years.

[tape ends]

British Bulldogs

The Irish pub is crammed with weekenders and reeks of damp clothes. Dingo must have a real thirst on him, as he's already leaning over the bar talking to the barmaid. I take my jacket off and run a hand through my wet hair. Tourists cluster round the tables in varying states of wastedness. Gilly has found a table against the back wall and they shuffle down into the low seats, McKirdy playing with his Rizlas.

The barmaid pours the third pint, and Dingo silently observes her like a cat peering into a fishtank. She starts on the fourth, and Dingo leans across the bar, picks up one of the froth-topped glasses and takes a gulp.

I slide up next to him at the bar. "Hey mate."

He glances over and then returns his attention to the pints. "Gaggin on a beer."

His wallet lies on the bar, flopped open. I'm surprised to see a picture of my sister and nephew neatly tucked into the plastic window. It's a recent photo: Ailsa started to grow her hair six months ago when they got engaged, and this is the longest I've seen it in years, down past her shoulders, natural chestnut colour instead of bottle blonde. She's grinning and holding Wee Calvin who points at the camera, or points at the photographer, who I'm guessing was Dingo. Ailsa looks happy, but in her smile is a hint of her childhood vulnerability.

I think back to one of Ailsa's favourite childhood games. She would dress up in our mother's clothes and jewellery and swish around the house, claiming she was rehearsing her future as a diplomat in Geneva. She was good at French, good at a lot of things. An uncharitable thought comes to me: I wonder if she's settling for less, marrying Dingo. The general consensus in Cloudburn is that Dingo – AKA Colin Dingwall – is *a disappointment*. I've heard all the condemnations over the years: from neighbours, schoolmates, teachers, Dingo's parents, local shopkeepers, the hairdresser, the Boys' Brigade leader (now serving in Saughton prison after being convicted of lewd behaviour with minors) and even the town drunks, slurring into their fortified wine.

A sigh, a shake of the head, and the verdict.

"Yon laddie's a waste eh space."

We were great friends when we were kids. We met on the first day of primary school, aged five. Class P1. I'm not sure if my recollections are real or have been fabricated from the ancient crayon and pencil scribbles of my diaries and the meandering legends spun by my mother. What is certain is that Dingo and me were inseparable. I remember us taking turns to kick a battered plastic football against the wall of the telephone exchange, our matching satchels with their aroma of leather and pencil shavings. A photograph in one of my mother's albums shows two boys with Bay

City Roller mops of hair, arms around each other, gappy smiles and skint knees. "Ye were like brothers," my mother proclaims every time she takes out the album, flattening the cellophane against the photo with her fingertip, stroking it reverently like a religious icon.

I remember us crawling through rhododendron caves searching for fairies, hands blackened by the mulchy ground, heart beating faster every time a twig snapped nearby. Chasing each other with sausages of dogshite speared on the end of sticks. Long summer nights of choreographed battles in our back gardens between massed armies of toy soldiers: an alliance of German infantry and Cowboys taking on the rebel forces of GIs, Red Indians, Space Rangers and the occasional plastic dinosaur that had escaped from the toybox in a fit of bloodlust.

The schism in our friendship began when we discovered Dingo was good at football and I was crap.

Age eight. Dingo was small and wiry and could shrug off challenges and get past other players like the ball was sewn to his ankle. He would score six or seven goals every playtime, squeeze the ball through jacket goalposts from ridiculous angles, acknowledge the invisible crowds with a raised finger.

I could toe-punt the ball over the playground wall while windmilling my arms. That was about it.

And so, at this early age, the food chain evolved, separating the predators from the prey. By virtue of his footballing skills Dingo became one of the alpha males in our year. The predators overlooked the fact that Dingo was a slow reader, pronounced his Rs as Ws, had girlish hair and galaxies of freckles all over his body. He had secured his place at the top thanks to his playtime goals.

I, on the other hand, was in the lower echelons. A tendency to wear my navy-blue anorak zipped up to my throat and carry dog-eared Tintin books everywhere I went had marked me out as something of an eccentric. I was happy to play on my own, aeroplaning around the school grounds with a Tintin book for each wing.

As primary school progressed, Dingo and I slowly settled into our different layers of the caste system and saw less and less of each other. We lived only three streets away, me in the council estate, Dingo in Cloudburn's new quarter of semi-detached houses arranged in neat crescents and avenues. By the time we got to the high school Dingo was emerging as a potential local hero. He was on the books of Dundee United and travelled up there twice a week to play for the youth team. Rumour had it that the head coach was predicting great things, and Dingo carried this promise with silent dignity, mumbling disclaimers every time anyone talked up his prospects.

Adolescence arrived in an eruption of pus and pubes. Dingo was one of the first, his voice breaking at age twelve, a caterpillar of wispy black hair on his upper lip. In the showers after PE the boys huddled or swaggered according to their pube-count. Classrooms stank of sweat and secret secretions. I decided it was time to grow up, hid my Tintin books in the attic, and started reading science-fiction and Tolkien instead. My fringe grew down over my eyes, partially obscuring my rabbit-in-the-headlights expression.

By the time my voice broke, Dingo had stopped growing. In the form class photograph for S4 Dingo stands at the end of the middle row, dwarfed by lanky boys and beanpole girls, his forced smile hinting his time at the top is over. Dundee United released him that summer, saying he was too small to make it as a professional footballer. The Cloudburn worthies rubbished this, pointing out all the great diminutive Scottish wingers, from Alex James right up to Kevin McAllister. But these reassurances made little difference. The dream was over.

So as I grew and grew and grew, reaching six foot two at age seventeen, Dingo and his reputation shrank. In fifth year he was caught cracking the window of the town police station with a concrete bollard while tanked up on cider; his clean record and the pleas of his middle-class parents saved him from serious punishment and earned him a £500 fine and a hundred hours of community service at the local old folks' home. In between playing Buckaroo with senior citizens and sitting through school in a catatonic daze, Dingo popped pills, smoked weed, swigged cider and avoided talking about football.

I read *Lord of the Rings* for the fourth time and passed my exams.

One day, during that last summer in 1991, just before my encounter with Morag in the archives, I bumped into Dingo outside the Co-op. He swigged from a glass bottle of Tizer and told me about his new job at the petrol station. His accent had got thicker since leaving school – he now spoke the dialect of the town's unemployed miners and factory workers.

"Mind eh the dogshite oan the sticks?" Dingo had said, grinning.

"Aye," I replied. "It was funny. Back then." And that was the last time we spoke, more or less for fourteen years, until he impregnated my sister.

At the bar, the silence is lengthening.

"It's a good photo." I nudge Dingo and point at the wallet.

He picks it up and looks at it as if he's seeing it for the first time. "Took it a couple eh weeks ago. The wee man's second birthday."

The barmaid gently places the pints in front of us and Dingo hands over a fifty.

I nudge Dingo. "Sorry for forgetting."

"Aye, yir OK. It's no like he's auld enough tae ken."

"How is he?"

"Aye, daein well. Growin up fast."

"And my Mum and Da? You see them much?"

"Every day." There is a trace of weariness in Dingo's voice.

"How about Ailsa?"

"Same as ever," says Dingo, and picks three pints up together in a two-handed grip and moves off towards our table. I collect the other pints and follow.

As I sit down at the end of a low bench I get a pang of guilt about Ailsa. Is there something wrong with me? While she's been planning her wedding, I've been fucking people whose names I don't know. How has it come to this? Is it all Eva's fault?

"So," says Razor. "Now we have pints, it's time for a wee bit eh stag chat. Questions about sex, n we aw have tae answer them – nae dodgin bullets."

"Aww min, no this," says Gilly.

Razor places a firm hand on the table. "It's part eh the stag experience. Whit happens in Amsterdam stays in Amsterdam, mind?"

"True dat," says McKirdy.

"Right," says Razor. He takes a cigarette out and spins it in the middle of the table, making it point – a little too obviously – at McKirdy. "Wee Stevie, you have tae answer first."

McKirdy nods solemnly.

Adopting the pucker tones of a gameshow host, Razor introduces the burning question. "Steven McKirdy. I have to remind you that you need to provide the answer within sixty seconds or face a forfeit. Are you ready? Here is the question. *What* – I repeat – *what* was your most embarrassing ever sexual fantasy?"

Rumbles and mumbles from the others, McKirdy cursing under his breath.

"Twenty seconds gone already. I can assure you that the forfeit will be far more embarrassing than answering the question."

McKirdy gulps from his pint.

"Only fifteen seconds remain. May I remind you that –"

"Whoopi Goldberg," says McKirdy.

The distillery boys collapse into cackles and heckles.

McKirdy motions to Razor. “Next. Cmon, spin the ciggy.”

“Ye must be fuckin jokin if ye think I’m answerin *that* question. Maybe ye can buy us another round, Stevie... maybe we’ll forget about Whoopi?”

McKirdy mutters something inaudible and hides his face in his pint.

I take another mouthful of lager, my pint already two-thirds gone. Around us in the bar, a gathering of umpteen wasted clans. Groups, mostly male, huddle round the low tables. They grin and holler, whisper conspiratorially, glance around suspiciously at the other groups. I tune in to the noise in the bar, the music surprisingly low, and manage to pick up several voices competing for attention. Welsh at the table next to us. Geordies two tables up. A Glaswegian somewhere, drawling “no wayyyyy, man! Fuckin bastard.” Londoners. West Country.

For all the regional and ethnic pride in our collection of North Sea islands, we’re all the fucking same. Bred over hundreds of years to fill our place in society. Genetically engineered by the Industrial Revolution to be squaddies, factory workers, office clerks, security guards, kitchen staff. Born to be suspicious of the people from the nearest town, from the social class above and/or below. Born to have our thirsts slaked with booze, our lungs filled with smoke, our arteries sludged with saturated fat, our dicks stuck in the girl next door.

Suddenly an avalanche of laughter interrupts the hubbub, and in perfect synchronisation, the distillery boys swivel round and glare at the offenders. The laughter subsides, but the accompanying voices stay at the same pitch, as if the volume controls are jammed. Oxbridge voices, at a table near the bar, five or six of them with their cheekily ruffled hair and rugby shirts. It seems that even these days the upper classes have been absorbed into the slum.

Razor returns with fresh pints and clunks them onto our table. “Fuckin loud posh cunts,” he says.

“Bunch eh cunts,” agrees Gilly. “But we’ve got mair important hings on oor minds.” He clutches his crotch and squeezes, pouts like a chimp.

Dingo picks up his pint and takes a slurp. Remembering the photo of Ailsa and Calvin in his wallet, I feel a rush of affection for him – he’s not going to misbehave this weekend. That’s my gut feeling. I’m glad he loves her, glad he looks after them.

“I’m aff tae feed the shitehawks.” Gilly gets up and walks across the pub. He stops in the middle of the bar, unsure where to go, and for a moment I fantasise he’s going to walk outside and fall into the canal and sink to the muddy bottom, subsumed into the centuries of rubbish layered in the clinging filth. If only. Gilly shouts at the barman, who points over to the corner, and he waves his thanks and totters off towards the toilet.

My pint is fizzy. I watch the bubbles congregate at the base of the glass and plume upwards through the middle of the golden liquid. It’s not Dutch beer – it has the look of British factory lager: slightly syrupy, over-carbonated, fortified with toxins to depress and enrage.

Will all this alcohol dull the pain if the psycho-pimp breaks my kneecaps later on? I have a vague memory of reading about wounded soldiers in the Crimean war drinking brandy before getting gangrenous limbs amputated. I rotate my pint glass, watch the fizz continue to rise. Part of me wishes the psycho-pimp would come through the door right now and just do whatever the fuck he wants to do. The way I feel at the moment, I would just close my eyes and take the hit.

Gilly returns to the table. "Fin. Yir a moody cunt, ih? Whit's up?"

Dingo cuts in before I can reply. "Cmon, Gilly. Gie it a rest."

"Had a tough week, that's all."

"Tough week ma arse. Workin in yir fancy office." Gilly grins. Unfocused eyes, he rocks slightly as he points at me. "Ye always were a snobby fucker at school. Wi yir alternative music n fancy books – better than the rest eh us, ih? But just a fuckin geek, that's aw."

"Shut your fucking hole."

He winks at me. "Just haein a wee joke, neebs."

Razor, slumped in his chair, begins to laugh. McKirdy looks like he's praying, leaning forward with his eyes closed, chin resting on his clenched hands. Those two are out the game already. The pub is busier now, people standing around the bar, music louder.

"I need tae gie Ailsa a quick call at some point," says Dingo.

Gilly slaps a hand on the table. "No ye fuckin dinnae. This is yir stag."

"Just a quick call," says Dingo. "I promised her, ken."

"Fuck, min." Gilly grips his forehead in his hand. "We're here tae skull drugs, fuck whores, get hammered before ye gie up aw yir freedom next week. Are ye fuckin insane?"

"It's just a call, Gilly. Dinnae get yir nuts in a twist."

"She'll no answer. She's probably gettin fucked by the binman," says Gilly. "Screamin for more."

The atmosphere in the bar has changed, as if someone opened an airlock at the back of the building and all the oxygen has whooshed out.

"That's my sister you're talking about." I stare at Gilly, willing him to meet my eye.

Gilly ignores both of us and continues to smile at Dingo.

"Ailsa's a nice piece, man. Ye think ye can leave her alone for a weekend without her wantin some cock?"

Dingo stares back at Gilly, clenching his teeth.

Gilly continues. "Dinnae take it the wrong way, likes. I'm just sayin. Ye havetae keep an eye oot, ken?"

Dingo grips his pint glass.

"Take me for example," says Gilly. "I'd love tae fuck Ailsa. Up the arse."

I make to stand up, but McKirdy's hand shoots out and presses into my chest, blocking me.

And now the noise has left the bar too. Maybe it's the lingering effects of the hash but all I'm aware of is Dingo's face, frozen, like someone has pressed pause.

Gilly launches himself upwards but Dingo, showing the turn of speed he had in his footballing days, is up first, and Gilly only succeeds in stepping into his punch.

Fast forward.

Gilly tumbles backwards into his chair and his flailing leg sweeps the drinks off the table and the clatter of the chair hitting the floor is followed by the slush and tinkle of smashing pints. Razor and McKirdy up on their feet, fully wakened, arms out to intervene. Gilly bounces back up, face a twist of blood and hate, and attempts to throw a punch at Dingo through the picket line of Rae and McKirdy. Dingo fights for a way through, and I grab him, hold him back – he wriggles and bucks like a landed fish.

The barman lunges over, and at that moment Razor and McKirdy successfully pin Gilly, restraining him with one arm each. I steer Dingo away from the table, and stoop to grab my jacket. Dingo sees his opportunity and lunges out at Gilly again, but this time the barman is in there, and flips Dingo into an armlock. The whole pub watches us, an audience of leering, excited faces. All part of the weekend's entertainment.

Gilly, struggling against Razor and McKirdy, opens his mouth. "Yir fuckin pathetic! Marryin a bird when ye urnae even the faither eh her kid!"

Dingo, despite being padlocked into the bouncer's grip, squirms in protest.

"That's right!" shouts Gilly as the bouncer leads Dingo slowly off the premises. "Wee Calvin! He's no your kid! I fucked Ailsa for three months behind yir back! Write a poem about that, ya cunt!"

Rain. Neon. The wind buffeting into us, the music behind us just a distant murmur. The barman releases Dingo and shoves him out into the road. Dingo is crying. Sniffling, shaking his twisted arm, mumbling to himself, chin slathered in spit.

"Now fuck off outta here," says the barman in a Dutch-American accent.

I grab Dingo and he pushes me away, then I try again, gentler, slip an arm around his shoulders. "Cmon mate. Gilly's talking shite. Trying to wind you up."

"Fuckin bastard," mumbles Dingo.

I lead Dingo over the nearest bridge and deeper into the heart of the red-light district. I'm not sure where I'm going, but I want to keep moving, want to be around people, disappear into crowds.

When we reach the other side of the canal Dingo's mobile chimes and he fumbles in his trouser pocket. He flips it open and thumbs the keypad, and for a moment I see his agonised face caught in the glow of the handset. He looks away and hands me the moby. The message is from Ailsa and reads:

HI SWEETIE HOPE
UR HAVING
FUN XXXOOO
A&WC

He snatches the phone back from me and in one fluid movement hurls it out above the canal. It arcs through the rain and drops into the water with a soft splish.

"It's fuckin over!" he screams.

Erotic Encounter Nos. 13-301 : Evil Fairies

[clears throat]

How do you summarise all the erotic encounters in a marriage? I'm struggling with this one, Eva. I'd never tell my mates about anything I did in a long-term relationship – a love relationship, unlike the pub chat about the casual stuff. Unless of course you think by its very nature marriage isn't erotic and there are only a handful of moments that warrant a mention. But I would disagree with that.

[noise of beer can opening]

Popping a tinny is my signature tune, right? My very own jingle. Ladies and gentlemen, the show is about to begin.

I'll start with the morning after that first night together. Jolted from sleep by an Edinburgh bus droning past. The shadowy light of early morning, Kathleen's clothes scattered around the room from her furious strip the night before, two torn condom wrappers dropped on the carpet. Lying there with her asleep next to me, enjoying her oblivion, enjoying the feeling of belonging. Twenty-four years old and forgivably flawed, my whole life in front of me for the taking. I remember thinking, even on that first morning, that this was going to be for life, that nothing would take this away from us.

Wine, videos and sex. That was the schedule for the first couple of months. I would finish work and head up to Kathleen's bedsit in Bruntsfield, usually stopping for a cheap bottle on the way. Her flatmate, who owned the place, was a restaurant manager and gone most evenings. It was a thrill to press the intercom buzzer and wait for the crackle, her voice calling me upstairs. Some evenings she would open the door naked and within seconds we would be entangled on her bed or the sofa or the floor. Other nights we would coorie up on her single bed and watch videos on her tiny portable TV, drinking wine out of teacups and eating nachos. At weekends we would relocate to the local pubs, or if the weather was decent, lie on the Bruntsfield Links with a boozy picnic. We didn't see much of our friends during that first long summer. I remember lots of comfortable silences, a gladness and shock that this was happening.

As the summer faded into autumn we decided to move in together and found a flatshare with another couple in Marchmont. Our living space was a huge bedroom filled with dusty furniture, the walls lined with fitted bookshelves. I got a new job with MacKenzie & Grierson, my first step into marketing, bringing with it a 20% pay rise. Kathleen wasn't too happy with her job at Scottish Standard but it was tolerable. Things were good.

We celebrated our first anniversary together by buying a flat. A one-bedroomed new-build in Fountainbridge not far from the brewery. The flat smelled of fresh paint and laminated wood but when you slid the double-glazed windows open the hoppy scent of fermenting beer crept inside. When I look back to this time – late '98 – I think of walking through the dark morning, hard frost glued to the pavements, clouds of steam drifting over from the brewery, going into the bakery for my morning roll, the sheen of bacon grease on the paper bag. I think about sex. Positioning myself behind Kathleen on the bed, her hand tucking me inside and banging hard into her, our thighs slapping. Her on top, grinding, eyes locked on mine.

On Kathleen's 25th birthday I took her to the Witchery restaurant on the Royal Mile and proposed to her over white chocolate cheesecake. We decided to have a small registry wedding, with a party at the Cloudburn distillery function room. It was a good day: blue skies, a buffet and a ceilidh. Kathleen wore a long-sleeved dress to cover the burns. My father spent most of the day staring at me suspiciously. I knew he didn't like what I was becoming – a flash, glitzy capitalist. I remember seeing Dingo and Ailsa dancing the Gay Gordons together and thinking nothing of it. I'd find out later they were already seeing each other.

Things were fine for seven years. People often commented that we were good together. Of course, we had the occasional disagreement, but we had common interests – cooking Indian food, hill-walking, jogging, pubs, movies, weekend city breaks. Holidays, dates, the occasional Sunday spent in bed. We started talking about kids, and around that time I probably started to take her for granted.

Autumn 2005. I should have seen the early signs that something was wrong, but I was too engrossed in work. I'd recently been appointed Marketing Manager for Cloudburn – my dream job, at last – and was spending late nights at the office, going through the latest concept briefs from design agencies, head filled with inspiration and confusion and back to inspiration again. Meanwhile, Kathleen had started teacher training and was on her first placement going through lesson plans and course materials. I'd come back around ten to find the living-room wall redecorated with yellow post-it notes, ring-binders open on the floor like mantraps. Make her tea, maybe pour her wine, then retreat to bed with a book. Sometimes I'd wake up in the middle of the night, alone in bed and notice a thin line of light at the bottom of the bedroom door. Most times I found her asleep on the sofa.

The sex dried up. We were too busy, too tired. It was acceptable in the short-term; we muttered apologies to each other, kissed and cuddled. What I didn't realise was that we'd stopped talking about anything except Cloudburn or teaching.

In November, the life we'd built together began to slip away.

I came home on a Friday night, excited because we'd signed off the new design for Cloudburn. I'd sent

Kathleen an email to say we'd celebrate that night. Her choice of food. No reply but I thought she was probably just too busy. I came home with a bottle of Chardonnay. She was sitting at the kitchen table, marking essays. No response to my greeting and when I got closer I saw that she wasn't marking the essays, just staring at them.

I'm having one of my dark spells, she said.

A few days into the New Year, she dropped out of teacher training. I tried to persuade her otherwise but she refused to talk about it. I phoned her mum and my mum. Ailsa came through to Edinburgh to talk to her, sometimes twice a week. I phoned the college administrator and explained the situation. They said they'd give her a couple of weeks to come back and if not carry her place over for next year. I told Kathleen she should maybe speak to someone about her depression – a professional.

She told me I just didn't fucking get it. She was right: I didn't get it. So I threw myself into work. She had never been enthusiastic about the teaching anyway – maybe it was for the best. She just needed time. She'd get through this and come out the other side a tougher person. This was what I told myself. I watched the Cloudburn redesign slowly take shape and promised myself I'd take her on a surprise holiday after it was all over.

She spent the days reading books and going to the cinema. Some nights I'd get back early and she'd cook a meal for us, we'd drink a bottle of wine and have sex, and I'd get the feeling things were returning to normal.

Other nights she'd not say a word, sit on the sofa with her knees tucked up to her chin.

When the spring arrived she seemed brighter. She was taking long walks around the city. I had my own troubles – quality issues with the new Cloudburn bottle. I spent one week down in Liverpool with the supplier and long days at the bottling plant in Paisley.

One night when I got back home she was in a really good mood. A smile like she was keeping a secret. Her good mood continued all week. She started to disappear in the evenings and I would find myself in the empty flat, sitting in silence save for the neighbours' TV chattering through the walls. She'd met somebody – I decided that was the only explanation. Somebody who was listening to all her problems, somebody who wasn't as detached as me.

One night she got back at midnight, closing the door quietly behind her. I was waiting at the kitchen table, still wearing my work clothes. She was startled.

I came right out with it and asked her if she was seeing someone else.

She laughed and said: *I am seeing someone but it's not what you think.*

I asked her who.

God, she said.

It was my turn to laugh.

She turned away, saying this was why she hadn't told me, but I grabbed her arm and after a brief tugging match, managed to ease her down onto the sofa.

Tell me. I hoped my voice was soft.

She explained.

It happened on one of her long walks. She was crossing the Meadows, watching her feet as the afternoon darkened, when a man stepped into her path, apologised and asked if she lived nearby. The way he stood in the middle of the path made her nervous but he was small and thin and unthreatening and lots of other people were walking by.

He wanted to tell her about his church. She let him talk, curious, wondering what kind of freaky cult he belonged to. But it didn't sound freaky at all. Christianity redesigned for the new millennium, he said, based on inclusiveness and respect, with love for the planet as important as love for all of humankind. He introduced himself as Hamish Urquhart, and amused, she shook his hand. What he wanted to know was – well, this was the thing – the Planetarian Church was looking for new members and he wondered if she would like to come and meet everyone. No pressure, just pop in and have a cup of tea and a biscuit and see if she feels at home. *Because*, he told her, *I saw you walking and you looked troubled.*

She went. Hamish suggested she sit in a corner and just absorb the energy. And as she sat there the miracle happened – she felt an overwhelming peacefulness. It started in her feet and tingled all the way up through her body and she stayed there for twenty minutes in a trance. All the tension left her. She forgot about everything. Realised that her fears and anxiety were exactly that – intangible emotions that could be untied and set free.

And since this *miracle* she'd been going there every day. She'd made good friends with the folk in the congregation. Especially Hamish. Wouldn't stop fucking talking about him.

[noise of empty beer can being crushed]

I was glad at first because she seemed happier. But in reality this was the moment the first cracks appeared. She would go to the church most days and try to persuade me to go too. I refused and threw myself into work even more than usual. The Cloudburn relaunch was coming up and I got invited by the American fanclub, the Cloudburners, to attend a sci-fi fantasy convention as their special guest. I asked Kathleen to come with me, paying for it out my own pocket but she said she wasn't ready for a big trip. So instead I turned the trip into business, organised my own stall at the convention to flog bottles of Cloudburn and t-shirts and shite like that. I flew over to Minneapolis at the end of September and checked into a motel adjoining the conference centre. The convention was a massive success – my pitch was between an orc body armour stall and a Deep Space 9 make-up artist – I got a few hundred names on the mailing list, sold out all 200 bottles and was just left with a few t-shirts. The Cloudburners were major fucking geeks but they were right into their whisky and really nice to me. We hit the local bars afterwards and I had my own wee entourage of nerds who were dead into all the Scottish stuff. I got stuck with this guy who kept asking me about the Dark

Isle. I had no idea what he was on about and then he told me it was Skye he meant, what was it like to stand there and watch the sea and feel the atmosphere. I told him I'd never been to Skye and he soon fucked off.

As the night drew on I got stuck with a redhead who was dressed up in a lizardwoman outfit. It was an impressive costume and really sexy – green scaly bodypaint all over, hotpants, bikini top, red contact lens and a sort of cape jacket thing. The geeks were in total awe of her and too shy to strike up a conversation – consequently I was the only one who chatted to her. Turned out we were staying in the same motel and we walked back together. Just as I was saying goodnight she made all these monster noises and flung herself at me. She got in my door and started fooling around and did a wee dance and was soon out of her top and wearing nothing except her hotpants – still doing her lizard dance while sticking her tongue out. She had green body paint all over, even over her boobs. She started rubbing against me but I was too shocked to be tempted and managed to get her out and locked the door.

It was my first close thing in terms of being unfaithful to Kathleen: the green paint smears on my arms and clothes were a reminder of just how close I'd come. I opened the windows and poured myself a dram of Cloudburn. The night was cold and just standing there looking out at the blackness you could feel that emptiness nearby. The prairies: all that emptiness, just a few miles away. I had the feeling I was on the edge of something massive that night, and right enough I would soon fall over the side.

[tape ends]

The Last Beer

The sharp clack of pool balls colliding wakes Dingo up.

He lurches up mid-snore, eyes staring madly, and looks around the bar with the awe and fascination of a two-year-old. "Where the fuck?"

"It's all right, Dingo. You're in Amsterdam, remember?"

Dingo continues to stare around the bar. I follow his gaze. The pub is L-shaped, and at the back the pool table is just visible through a huddle of bodies. The barmaid glances over, hands on hips. Above her an illuminated Heineken sign gives the bar a greenish glow. The clock on the wall reads ten past eleven. Spike's bar is on the fringes of the red-light district, away from the main drag, on the edge of respectability but still tainted with a sleaziness that hangs in the air like radiation.

My beer is flat and warm. I bought the round half an hour ago. After Gilly's terrible declaration, I dragged Dingo around a succession of bars, insisting at first that he drank cola. *Gilly's talking shite.* I offered this again and again, because the thought of Ailsa sleeping with Gilly is so beyond the pale that it's almost comical. But Dingo's face betrayed something else, an emptiness in his eyes that suggested doubts confirmed. Over Guinness in Molly Malone's I'd repeated my mantra again – *Dingo, listen mate, he's talking shite* – and Dingo grabbed my arm and told me to stop. With conversation banned, I took him to a coffeeshop, where we bought a pre-rolled and killed half an hour. As we shared the joint I remembered the words from his poem – *sting of love, missing flower* – and the green and blue lights blurred and sharpened, like the tectonic plates of the universe were shifting.

Dingo rubs his eyes, takes a mouthful of beer and fixes me in his stare.

"Is this yir life, Fin?"

"What do you mean?"

"Aw this drinkin, druggin n hoorin. Is this just a normal weekend?"

"Of course not."

Dingo rocks back on his chair and tilts his head towards the ceiling. "Ye cannae wait tae get rid eh me, right?"

"What?"

"Get rid eh me then go back tae yir life in yir nice wee flat, pretendin that none eh us exist, that Cloudburn doesnae exist."

"What the fuck, Dingo."

"Cmon. I saw it in yir face the moment ye met us. Aloof. Switchin between different lives like a fuckin conman."

I take a mouthful of beer. "Fucksake, Dingo. You think it's easy for me, seeing these Cloudburn lads again? Rae used to bully me. And I can't stand the sight of Gilly."

Dingo picks at his beermat.

I go for broke. "Being totally honest now. I'm worried. I'm crapping myself. Maybe it's the ganja, but I'm freaking out. I just need to understand what's going on, what Gilly said –"

Dingo is crying. He's trying to hide it behind a wince, but his eyes brim over and tears slide down his face and under his chin. "I love her so much. I love Wee Calvin so much."

"I know that."

"But I dinnae deserve them."

"You do. My Mum thinks the sun shines out your bahookie."

He slurs his words. "I'm a failure. They deserve better."

"You're not a failure."

Dingo scoffs. "Cmon, Fin. At least have the decency tae tell the truth."

"You're not the failure Dingo. I am."

"Fuck off, golden boy."

I almost spill my beer. "It's the truth. I'm divorced and I'm going to lose my job."

"Eh?"

Cheers and laughter from through the back of the pub – black ball potted.

"It's true." I have a feeling this might make Dingo feel better. "I found out at work before coming to meet you. Cloudburn is in a bad way. Sales are terrible. They want to get rid of the Curse stuff, try something else."

Dingo shrugs. "Maybe that's a good thing."

"What do you mean?"

"Well, someone'll find out sooner or later that it's all a load eh shite, right?"

"A load of shite?"

"Aye, aw the made up stuff."

I pick up my beer then put it down again. "Made up stuff?"

"Aye," says Dingo. "The Bottle of Brotherhood for starters."

"What do you mean?"

Dingo laughs, the first time I've seen any emotion other than despair on his face for a while. "Come on, Fin. Ye dinnae believe it's really whisky from the first cask? A gift from one brother to another on his deathbed?"

"Well... I do."

He laughs again. "Some of the older boys at the distillery say it was a clever wee fib in the fifties. They just took some regular spirit and banged a pretend old label on the bottle."

I shift in my seat. "But the Curse of Cloudburn –"

Dingo smiles. "When ye compiled the tour guide notes where did ye get yir information fae?"

"*The Curse of Cloudburn* book. You know that."

"It's about as true as Braveheart and the Loch Ness Monster combined."

"But I also talked to Tavish Barclay. He said it was mostly true."

Dingo laughs. "Of course! Local historian Tavish Barclay. Such a reliable source."

I frown into my beer.

After finding *The Curse of Cloudburn* in the distillery storeroom in the summer of '91, I decided to take it to Tavish Barclay for verification. He was a bit of a bogeyman in Cloudburn. He lived in a rundown cottage on the Stirling Road, a couple of windows boarded up. Barclay himself was similarly dilapidated, with wild white hair and a waxy body odour that Da claimed could clear The Drookit Dug in under a minute – until, that is, the landlord banned him for his negative impact on business. Barclay had written numerous books on Scottish history, focusing on obscure subjects such as the jute industry, sheep breeds, and Scottish emigration to Argentina. His most recent title at the time was *Displaced Doric: the influence of Aberdeenshire Migrants on the Dialect of Cloudburn.* Not a big seller, needless to say.

The day I visited his cottage, I almost changed my mind at the last minute. The pavement outside had been defaced with chalk scrawls: circles around droppings of dogshit and messages such as *WOULD YOU LEAVE THIS MESS OUTSIDE YOUR OWN HOUSE YOU PIG.* I knocked softly on the door, half-hoping he wouldn't hear. But the door swung open, and a musty odour came out to welcome me. Tavish Barclay wore a pullover patterned with soup stains.

"What are you selling, and what makes you think I'll be interested?" he said.

I told him I had some questions about Cloudburn's history. His face lit up and he ushered me in. The house was dark and the walls were hidden by leaning stacks of books. A cat dashed underfoot and Barclay offered me a seat, settled down into an ancient armchair and said it was important to always start at the beginning. He waffled for two hours. I scribbled notes and interrupted him with questions in the few moments of silence. I returned three more times, until I had the answer to all my questions, and gave him a bottle of Cloudburn for his troubles. His told me to come back whenever I wanted. I last encountered Tavish about five years ago, walking across the plaza with Mum. I smelled him before I saw him. "Why if it isn't Young Findlay!" He told me he was writing his latest book on the sex life of Rob Roy McGregor. I kept it quick before my mother, thirty years a nurse, stripped him and shoved him headfirst into the nearest bath.

Dingo sips his beer. "Tell me where the distillery's water source goes. Whit does it say in *The Curse of Cloudburn*?"

The words are carved into the walls of my skull. "*MacLeod's Burn, the source of the distillery's water, disappears underground at the foot of Fairy Glen. Nobody knows where the water goes, although legend has it the burn flows through a network of underground caves before merging with the River Forth at Stirling.*"

"Rubbish!" Dingo is animated now, sitting up in his chair. "A couple eh weeks ago there was a blockage in the Cloudburn Tunnel, leaves n branches n stuff. We got some council guys in tae have a look n they crowbarred off the grille tae the tunnel. I asked these boys whit they saw underground. Contrary tae whit it says in the all-knowing book the tunnel is no mysterious underground ravine, but constructed fae Victorian brick. The tunnel then joins another, at which point it starts tae fuckin stink. Because here's what happens tae the distillery's water source – it connects wi the town sewer approximately under the bingo hall n assists in washin away the shite n pish eh the proud citizens eh Cloudburn."

"Sewer?"

"Aye, the sewer. No exactly the sort eh thing ye want the tourists tae find oot, is it?"

"So..." I rub my eyes, feeling suddenly very drunk. "The story about the Bottle of Brotherhood..."

"Utter mince."

"What really happened?"

Dingo shrugs. "Heard a few stories. Auld Tam in the bond says that the Skene brothers invested unwisely n then the Wall Street Crash fucked them. They sold up to Grierson Groceries."

"Fuck." I tip back more beer. "Why has nobody said anything about this? It's been more than fifteen years we've been running with the Curse stuff."

Dingo shrugs. "There's nae big conspiracy theory at work here. The only folk interested are the consumers n most eh them are Yanks. They *want* tae believe it n that's aw that matters."

"Fuck."

"Sorry, Fin. I didnae want tae pish on yir bonfire, but it's the truth."

Dingo's expression darkens and he reaches for his beer. I suspect he's just remembered Gilly.

The Curse of Cloudburn: fiction? I always took it for granted that the basic facts were correct – that the Skene children had died in circumstances tragic or mysterious enough that a legend could be woven around them. I would have guessed maybe 70% of it was bullshit. But it's 100% premium crap. Troll and pixie shit indeed. Maybe Newt was right.

"Let's go home."

Outside the rain has stopped, although the wind is still strong, whipping down the street, scattering scraps of litter and a crushed beer can. Dingo is silent as we walk, hands embedded in the pockets of his cargo pants, shivering. We cross the red-light district and cut over the Damrak, and onwards along Nieuwendijk and into the Jordaan. Just as we cross the Singel, the oldest of the city's canals, Dingo speaks.

"Gilly's got the spare keys."

I say nothing in reply. The night can barely get any worse.

The only sound as we walk is the scuffing of our feet on the pavement and the furling sail noise of Dingo's trouser legs rubbing together. Prinsengracht. We turn down onto the cobbled street, the Noorderkerk's stunted steeple leading us home.

I slow as we turn into Lindenstraat and slip my key between two fingers as an improvised knuckleduster. Come ahead, psycho-pimp. I've got nothing to lose.

The street is empty.

I unlock the front door and edge it open. The cliff-face staircase is as daunting as ever. As I step inside my foot brushes against something on the floor. A piece of paper. It's too dark to see what it is, so I pocket it and slowly climb the stairs, softly pressing my feet onto every step to minimise the noise. I reach the top of the stairs and peer around the living-room: no Gilly. The kitchen: no Gilly. I check the upper floor as well, the bedroom, the bathroom, the toilet, even the storage cupboard in the narrow hallway. No Gilly.

Back in the bright light, feet on the smooth wooden floors, I unfold the piece of paper and read the message, scrawled in bold capitals:

I'LL BE BACK YOU FUCKER

"Dingo!" I pass him the note. "Is this Gilly's writing?"

Dingo squints at the note and shrugs. "Dinnae ken. But his bag's still here." Both their bags lie in a mess of empty bottles. He leans back on the sofa again, folds his arms, hugs himself, closes his eyes.

I look at the note again and drop it onto the table. Right now I'm too tired and too drunk to care. I take the sleeping bag out of the cupboard and drape it over Dingo, who is already asleep.

My first day as his protector is over.

Erotic Encounter No.302: God

[a sigh, followed by noise of beer can opening]

After I got back from Minneapolis I was in for a surprise.

Kathleen told me she'd decided to *cleanse* herself for a year.

Turned out this church of hers recommended a path to God: no booze, ciggies, drugs, TV or sex for three hundred and sixty-five days. After this *cleansing* she would be renewed and ready to begin her new life. She held my hand and *implored* me to follow her on a path to God.

It was a difficult first night back. I kipped on the sofa.

Things went downhill fast. I said I wasn't going to join her on her path to God and she said she would be patient with me. She went to her church most evenings and with me at work during the day, we didn't see much of each other until the weekends. We were sleeping in the same bed but she wouldn't let me touch her or even cross the invisible line between us. She was still cordial enough, but the Kathleen I knew was disappearing fast.

One day when I was at work she re-organised the flat, moving everything sinful to the spare room – the TV, DVD, whisky, CDs etcetera – and turned the living-room into a sort of meditation space. The map of our marriage was being re-drawn and it was clear who would be losing territory. Soon enough I started watching TV in the spare room then having a wee drink in the spare room and finally kipping on the sofa-bed in the spare room.

From your point of view, Eva, it must seem ridiculous – why not just walk away? But you have to remember we were married. I loved her. Kathleen was good friends with Ailsa. I was embarrassed by what was going on and didn't really want folk to find out. I was also obsessed with work again: late hours, ideas tearing through my head like comets, the sales figures for Cloudburn nudging closer and closer to what had seemed like impossible targets just six months before.

Kathleen's *cleansing* had gone on for about three months – then came the next surprise.

Over soup one night she told me that part of the process of recovery was to address *residual negative emotions*.

I tried to be funny. *You mean 98% of the Scottish personality?*

This isn't a joke, Fin. Fuck, the scariness of her eyes.

She told me that she had to overcome her depressive tendencies, cure her lack of self-esteem. To do this she was going to get out of her comfort zone and help a recently released prisoner integrate back into society.

All I remember is distant traffic noises outside and thinking *Aye she's finally gone loopy now.*

Kathleen suggested I should confront my own issues. I asked her what she meant. Again, the scary eyes. She stayed calm, staring at me, and explained that everyone has their own journey and it's unhelpful to make comparisons. I put my shoes on and left the flat, slamming the door on my way out.

We argued for a week, until finally we reached a compromise. I would go with her to see this recently released prisoner. It turned out Hamish was already going – it was him who'd offered the Planetarian Church's services to a rehabilitation charity. The ex-prisoner was called Campbell, had been jailed for assault, and lived in a bedsit in the Gorbals. I wasn't sure who I felt more like murdering: Campbell or Hamish.

So one Saturday Hamish turned up outside our flat in his beaten up Citroen Saxo. Funny looking guy: petite, well-groomed, with one of those beards that matched the length of his hair to the exact millimetre, like a fucking wraparound carpet. Precisely the kind of clothes I'd expected – expensive fleece and beige hiking trousers with zip-off legs. I sat in the back of the car on the journey through, staring at him while the marketer's voice in my head ran through insults I could brand him with. *God gimp. Sinister minister. Priest with the least.* And all the while the two of them sat in the front talking about *the next step* and *overcoming residual emotions* and pish like that.

Campbell's flat wasn't far from the Clyde on a litterblown street of brown tenements. Pure Glasgow gothic: black streaks of damp on the buildings and a dead cat in the undergrowth of his front garden. He buzzed us in – my heart was already going like the clappers. Up the stairs, Kathleen walking next to Hamish and me a couple of steps behind, feeling like the hired muscle rather than the husband.

The door opened. Campbell was a tragic wee fuck: the prison stint had obviously broken him. Terry-towelling tracksuit and a pint of milk in his hand, different lengths of stubble on his face. I stopped wanting to murder him as soon as I saw the state he was in.

Hamish took over. We sat in the living-room while he explained he was the *mediator* and the purpose of this meeting was to *facilitate a new pathway in life*. Kathleen was nervous and suddenly I felt my old love for her again – until that is, she said she was uncomfortable with me being in the room and asked if I could wait in the corridor.

The flat's decor was untouched since the seventies: flock wallpaper, burgundy and orange carpets, and glass-panelled doors. I stood in the corridor watching them through the glass. I couldn't hear what they were saying, just the murmur of conversation. Hamish's monotone droned on throughout. I imagined smashing my fist through the glass. Just to see their faces.

Kathleen was quiet for most of the journey back. Hamish kept his eyes on the road while explaining that the confusion she felt was part of the *challenge*, part of the fucking *journey*, and came out with some other pish about Jesus's love being *the healing salve for the most serious of wounds*. I just stared at him and wondered what right the fucker had interfering in other people's pain. I was glad when he dropped us off that Kathleen didn't invite him in. She seemed exhausted and I hoped this would be the end of it.

A few days passed. I lay awake in the spare room at nights fantasising about the green lizard woman in Minneapolis. An alternative life.

Then things got even worse. Kathleen told me Campbell had moved through to Edinburgh and had started coming to their church on part of his own *journey*, and she would be his mentor. It was *a blessing* that her journey would not only heal herself but another person too.

Now the rage really kicked in.

The financial year had closed and the new design of Cloudburn had beaten the sales target by 12%, and I had a number of parties to attend. For a couple of weeks I was scooting around Edinburgh going to bars and restaurants. The alcohol industry likes to think of its employees as ambassadors for responsible drinking but the truth is it cultivates a high percentage of alcoholic employees. So I was flavour of the month and all the senior managers wanted a piece of me – a great excuse to get the company credit card out and blow a few hundred on a good bevvy.

One such summer night I was up in the Tollcross area when I spotted Kathleen on the other side of the road. She was standing at the pedestrian crossing with

Hamish and Campbell. They were engaged in serious discussion. Campbell had tidied himself up a bit and wore a cheap suit. I followed them to the community centre that doubled as their church. I hid behind a van. They stood outside with a few others in the sunshine. Someone came out with a tray of drinks in polystyrene cups. I felt like going over there and knocking the tray over in their faces but instead I went back to meet my colleagues and drank till closing time.

That was the beginning of a bad habit. I started going to the pub opposite their church. The seat near the door gave a good view onto the building and sometimes I could make out Kathleen's head through the window. By the time I'd had a couple of pints they would all spill out onto the street, hanging around chatting if the weather was OK. One thing remained consistent – wherever Kathleen was, Hamish was just a few steps away. Campbell hung around on the edges of the group and usually left first.

Then one night Kathleen came out and a minute later Campbell exited and headed in the same direction. I drained my pint and slipped out into the street. It was late summer, starting to get dark. I followed Campbell and it was clear he was following Kathleen, going down through Tollcross and on into Fountainbridge. I sprinted ahead and took a sidestreet so I could cut Campbell off. It was back: that urge to murder the wee fuck.

I slowed so that I wouldn't shock him. Out I stepped, quite close to the brewery in a quiet part of the street. It was only when I was a few feet away that he seemed to register me. Something in his eyes saw what I was going to do before I even knew myself.

I got him by the throat and spun him into the wall. I gave him a good going over: a punch in the guts, a knee in the face then a few boots when he was on the pavement. He curled up like a hedgehog and stayed like that, moaning. I was buzzing, months of frustration boiling out of me. A car slowed to see what was going on and I turned back down the sidestreet, sprinted for a bit, cut down another street, and walked quickly home.

My hands were shaking and I couldn't get the keys in the lock. Kathleen heard me and opened the door. *He was following you*, I told her. *Fucking Campbell was following you.*

She said: *What did you do to him?*

This is what I'm ashamed of. This next bit.

I grabbed her. Hugged her but not in a romantic way. She struggled against me and then we were up against the wall, and I was pushing hard against her. I was turned on. You know. And she stopped struggling and looked me in the eye and asked if I was going to rape her.

[a few seconds of silence]

I let her go. She ran away to the spare room and slammed the door. I went to the bathroom. The world spun. I masturbated into the sink and sat on the edge of the bath and cried.

[tape ends]

SATURDAY

Extracted from www.cloudburn.com

On the rain-lashed, rocky slopes of the Ochil Hills, in the heart of what was once Scotland's most lawless county, a whisky of unparalleled distinction has been crafted for more than a hundred years. A whisky's character is always the sum of its ingredients, and Cloudburn's excellence is founded on purest springwater, the finest Scottish barley, and thirteen years of distilling in fine oak casks – through which the spirit absorbs the untamed air of the Scottish Highlands. Cloudburn Single Malt whisky's undisputed eminence has seen it win prizes and connoisseurs on every continent.

Yet it is not only its majestic taste that makes it so special. There is another, more sinister reason for its uniqueness – but before we explore Cloudburn's dark secret let us first savour the quality of the spirit.

Uncork the bottle and hold it under your nose – you will be overwhelmed by the sweet fragrance of summer wheatfields, the freshness of Atlantic rainclouds, and an underlying aroma of wood-smoke. Next, tip a few splashes of the golden spirit into your favourite glass. Raise it to your lips and allow the nectar to trickle between your teeth and into your mouth. Close your eyes and puddle the liquid on your tongue – experience the sweet sourness of wild brambles, the tingling warmth of Thai chilli, an earthy note of oatmeal and a surprising yet not unwelcome hint of seaweed.

Swallow, and enjoy the rich aftertaste – we guarantee you will already be contemplating a second glass.

As you enjoy the lingering glow from your dram of Cloudburn, consider now the second reason for this whisky's uniqueness – and try not to cough it back up.

Every time you raise a glass of Cloudburn to your lips, you are risking your future. Like all the best things in life – fast cars, free love, rock n'roll –this whisky is dangerous, but not because of anything your doctor tells you. Every mouthful of Cloudburn Single Malt Whisky is cursed.

Cloudburn is a whisky like no other – a whisky to die for.

Dreams of Black Fungus

I'm dreaming about black fungus.

Or, to be specific, *Torula compniacensis richon*. I memorised the Latin name as an eighteen-year-old – not for any academic reason, but because I was a teenage smart-arse.

My tour guide spiel echoes somewhere in my head. *Torula compniacensis richon, also known as Angel's Breath, is a black fungus that grows on the walls of whisky bonds. The fungus thrives on the alcohol vapour in the air and blackens the walls of the warehouses, inside and out, as well as nearby trees and buildings...*

The dream begins at the distillery. It's deserted, and the quality of light is bright and bleached, as if Cloudburn was in the Nevada desert rather than on the rainy faultline between the Scottish Lowlands and Highlands. I stand in the empty car park, blinking into the light. The wind whistles through the nearby buildings, creaks the tree branches, blows crisp bags across the tarmac. The main building, normally pristine, whitewashed twice a year, is hidden under a thick layer of black fungi. It covers the walls, windows, roof – much thicker than the usual smudges. I walk over to the building and see that up close the fungi is bunched in ugly blossoms, and closer still, made up from tangled spores resembling tiny filaments of blackened metal not unlike the shavings of steel I remember from the floor of the Technical Education classroom in Cloudburn High School. Strangely, the fungi stinks of booze puke, and as soon as I notice this, the stink is everywhere, rancid alcohol and bile, invading my mouth and nose and throat.

I turn and look back towards the car park, and see the fungi spreading as I stand, dotting the tarmac like black snow. Panic takes over, and I run towards the town, sprinting out the entrance and down the slip road. As I run I pick up speed until my legs start to pedal air, and I take off, flying. I tilt my body forwards and swoop up, twenty metres high, brushing a crow on the way. More crows – scraps of whirling black – flutter over me. I speed through the air for thirty seconds and slow above the new houses in town, the aerial view showing a neat grid of avenues, brown-tiled roofs and squared off gardens. I drift to the ground, and land softly on an overgrown lawn.

I am suddenly barefoot and the stubbly grass prickles the soles of my feet. The house in front of me is box-like, a delicate cream colour, the same as every other house on the street. Above it, high in the distance, the skies are heavy with what looks like black snow falling. The fungus. I rush towards the front door.

I step into silence and the smell of air-freshener and vegetable soup. Along the corridor is another door, light pine in colour, and behind it I can hear murmuring, giggling, thumping. I glide across the floor, ghost-walking, and pass through the door into a brightly lit kitchen.

Ailsa is naked, bent over the kitchen table, her blissful face resting on a scrunched up tablecloth. Gilly is behind her, hands clenching her hips, whacking himself steadily into her. He winks at me without breaking momentum. I hear a crunch behind me and turn to see Wee Calvin standing in the arched entrance to the living-room, his bare feet trampling spilled cornflakes.

The house trembles, wet black splats blossom on the window. The fungus is coming, avalanching from the skies, drumming on the roof and walls, and still Gilly and Ailsa thump away, Ailsa whooping, Gilly writhing like a rodeo cowboy.

The walls change colour, spores smudging the Orchid White wallpaper, darkening to black as I watch. It spreads to Ailsa and Gilly, bruising and furring their skin, spreads onto the linoleum, creeping across the floor like spilt ink. I am still untouched. Ailsa and Gilly have stopped moving, cocooned now in black webbing, frozen in the position of their final copulative moment: a Pompeii death-fuck. Out the window the black snow has drifted almost to the top of the window and it's getting difficult to breathe through the stink of booze and bile.

Wee Calvin still stands in the cornflake crumbs, like me strangely untouched by the black spores. He tilts his head upwards and meets my gaze, his grey eyes blank, and the drumming of the falling fungus becomes muffled, suggesting that the house is now entombed.

The electric light overhead casts a ghostly glow in our underground cave. Wee Calvin continues to stare at me and I notice a tiny speck on his cheek, just a blackhead, growing bigger, pea-sized, and bigger still, the size of a plum stone. Black bruises appear on his arms and all across his face and he gasps out a sob and suddenly there is no air left in the room, only stink and spores, and I choke and fall backwards onto the hard floor and slither and wriggle in the fungal muck, using my last breath to scream and yell and –

I bolt upright and the duvet slides off the bed and flumps to the floor.

Wee Calvin.

Ailsa.

It takes a few seconds for the panic to fade. As the dream recedes, reality floods into the vacuum. The dry ache of a hangover. The noises of the world outside my apartment. I sit up in bed and listen to the Saturday symphony. The throttled buzz of a moped on a nearby street. The distant hubbub of the market, only one street away but softened by the double glazing, laughter and bartering and greetings and goodbyes stirred together into a fuzz of soft static. Pigeons coo and flap and peck on the flat roof next to my window.

I take a deep breath and smell the booze and bile stink of my black fungus nightmare. Did I puke last night? I check the bed and floor but they're clean. Get out of bed and hobble into the hallway, naked except for my boxer shorts. Through the porthole window, I see my neighbour ironing a red shirt. I nudge open the toilet door – clean. The bathroom – clean. Clump down the stairs to the living-room, half-expecting to see it blackened by the fungus.

But the living-room is clean – and empty. Dingo's sleeping bag lies crumpled on the sofa like a shrugged-off exoskeleton. A mug lies on its side on the floor with a puddle of milky tea splashed nearby. The TV is on. BBC1 and the sizzle and hiss of a celeb chef grilling lamb chops.

"Dingo?"

No reply. The kitchen is also empty. I inspect the spilt tea closer up and dab my fingers in the splash of liquid: cold to the touch. Not much tea, like he maybe kicked it over when he stood up and didn't notice, entirely possible with the hangover he must have. Where is he? I scan the room and see that his bag is still here. Out for a bottle of juice? Or did the psycho-pimp get him?

After pacing around for a few minutes I realise I need something to distract me. Porridge. I go into the kitchen, slosh water into a saucepan, and add oatmeal. I turn the gas on and spark the lighter – *WHUMPH* – and it catches, flaring up in a fiery blossom, calming into a blue flower of flame. The roar of the gas is the only noise in the apartment.

The events of last night crawl back to me, blurred and misshapen. I replay the moment when Dingo smashed his fist into Gilly's face, and when he hurled his mobile into the canal. Neon and rain. I try to remember our conversation in Spike's Bar but the only part that remains clear is what Dingo told me about the Curse of Cloudburn. A load of old shite, basically.

The saucepan lid rattles gently, and I lift it off and stir the porridge. The water clouds and thickens as I whirl the spoon around. I turn the flame down low – a blue flower with the petals plucked – and keep stirring. A thud trembles through the building. After a few seconds I realise it was just my neighbour closing his door, but I'm shaking, jumped up to fuck. I need to keep busy and forget all the calamities. I slop the porridge into a bowl and return to the living room.

I eat my porridge, then go for a shower and shave. When I return downstairs there is still no sign of Dingo. My nightmare is still vivid, and for a brief moment I get a vision of black fungus raining on Amsterdam, sliding off the roofs and splattering onto the cobbles. My insides churn with dread. I can't shake the feeling that something terrible has happened – Dingo has run away, or something worse. Something to do with the psycho-pimp.

I need another distraction. Heart beating fast, I find a pen and a scrap of paper. At the top I scrawl NEW STRATEGY FOR CLOUDBURN. I stare at the blankness and try to concentrate. After a few minutes, I go to the fridge for a bottle of Grolsch. The white page looks back at me.

Once, the knowledge that I manufactured convincing legends gave me a glow of invincibility. My re-telling of an old story had crafted a whisky brand visible in thousands of drinks cabinets around the world, visible on thousands of supermarket shelves, visible on thousands of bar gantries. And perhaps more satisfying, the invisible manifestations of my creation – the people that absorbed my words, people on every continent who loved my hometown's whisky and its personality. I used to summon them, genie-like, to fulfil my wishes. The commuter stuck in the Tokyo rush hour – daydreaming of uncorking the bottle of Cloudburn when he gets home, the clunk of ice cube striking crystal. The Birmingham headmistress at the school assembly, imagining her nightly glass of Cloudburn and its taste of serenity. The computer geeks in an attic room in a snowblown Midwestern town, sipping Cloudburn as they listen to thrash metal and roleplay online. These genies followed me around, whispered encouragement in my ear. But today, they are silent; trapped in the bottle.

I finally give up after an hour, with only two scribbled ideas to show for my efforts:

New campaign based on name - flaming clouds, burning skies?

Minimalist Scottish Zen - lower case brand name, samurai swords, ninja stars, oriental tartan fusion label

My attention is drawn to the cabinet and the sixteen bottles of Cloudburn and I go over and take out a bottle of 1998 Distiller's Edition and pour two fingers. I stick my nose in the glass and sniff. The malt aficionados are fond of 18 Year Old Cloudburn: vanilla and spice they say it tastes of, with traces of something harder. Wasabi. Grapefruit.

Hard glass against my lips, I tip it back and the spirit trickles into my mouth. I let it puddle, swill it around and swallow. My tastebuds tingle and roar from the spikiness, saliva ebbs onto the back of my tongue. The liquid slips down my gullet and spreads its warmth into my blood.

It's been two hours since I came down the stairs to find the flat empty and Dingo absent. The silence is thickening around me, closing in. I stand up, then sit down again. Awful memories come back to me, of times I thought I had put behind me. Of Kathleen looking at me with empty eyes. Scotland fizzling and fading around me, until the only answer was to disappear before Scotland did.

The dread builds into an overwhelming sensation that someone is going to come for me soon. I lace my boots up and write a note to Dingo, telling him to meet me in The Nova Scotia at five o'clock, and stick it on the fridge. Rain drums on the window. I remember that we only have one set of keys, leave the door unsnibbed and step out into the greyness.

A rush of cold October air and the tinkle of a bicycle bell. I am overwhelmed by the sensation of Amsterdam: even at moments like this, I'm shocked that the Hansel and Gretel rooftops are not part of some delusion, some waking dream, and that I will surely wake with a jolt in stale sheets in an Edinburgh bedsit.

The market is in full swing, and crowds flow around the tightly packed stalls. Voices yell, bodies jostle, cyclists attempt slow-motion zig-zags through the throng. A gypsy lament rises up above the noise. Two buskers on the corner, one with a clarinet and the other an accordion. The plaintiveness of the lament rattles down my spine and makes my skin prickle. Like the Celts, these Roma know how to break your heart with a tune. As I pass them I delve a two euro coin out my pocket and drop it into the yawning accordion case with a clink. The accordionist grins at me revealing brown and gold teeth. Give me some luck today, mate.

Erotic Encounter No.303: The Norwegian Temp

[noise of beer can opening, followed by a sigh]

So after the night I beat up Campbell I woke to find Kathleen gone. That evening Hamish came round, standing there in a corduroy suit with his trimmed beard and aura of smugness. I had to restrain myself from kicking his fucking carpeted bonce in. He told me Campbell had a cracked rib and two broken fingers but didn't want to press charges. Campbell saw it as part of his own journey, part of his own *cleansing*.

Kathleen, he explained, wanted to give me a letter. I read it while Hamish stood there. She wanted a divorce. Wanted me out the flat. Still loved me but realised we could never be together. Hamish started to talk and I slammed the door in his face.

I moved out to a friend's place in Leith: a pokey wee room that looked onto the port. It was depressing to be honest. In that part of town all the stonework looks stained with oil or fish. Bookies all around and jakeys everywhere. Leith has the feel of a town parachuted into a city: a state within a state. Kosovo. Lesotho.

As for the whole Kathleen business, the worst was yet to come. I wasn't proud of it, but I'd started going to the pub opposite her church again. Stalking her basically. One evening I saw her and Hamish come out together, and as they walked up the street, she slipped her hand into his. I watched them until they turned the corner and stayed in my seat staring at my empty glass. The stalking stopped after that.

[pause, voice quieter when resumes]

Anyway, I want to talk about this sex I had. That's what I'm supposed to do, right?

It was maybe four or five months after splitting with Kathleen. I was working too hard and drinking too hard. The Cloudburn launch had gone well and the results from the previous quarter – end of 2006 – were the best ever. Then one afternoon an invitation got sent to the whole office for a meeting in the canteen.

There were loads of rumours in the build-up. A change of Managing Director, a new acquisition, maybe we were selling a brand? Three o'clock arrived and everybody shuffled into the canteen.

MacKenzie himself was there to tell us the news. The board had accepted a bid from their rival Stalwart to buy the company. It was regrettable but operations would move to Amsterdam and the Edinburgh office would close. There would be the opportunity to apply for jobs in the Amsterdam office but not many roles would be available. Redundancy payments would be made. The company regretted this outcome but it was inevitable.

The Human Resources department would have sessions with staff in the coming week to explain the next steps and answer any questions.

Someone threw a coffee mug and it smashed on the wall above MacKenzie's head. He flinched. Angry shouts and a general clamour with some people crying. I just sat there. It was enough already that Kathleen had dumped me; I'd burned up all my emotions. People started to leave. Some kicked over chairs on their way out. I went back to my desk, but soon gravitated over to the coffee area where a crowd had gathered. The conversation was predictably emotional – *whit about ma fuckin mortgage? They management cunts'll be OK. This business belongs in Scotland for fucksake.* Etcetera. At quarter to four the inevitable happened: someone proposed the pub and a mass exodus commenced.

We went to a pub I'd always hated, All Bar One on Lothian Road. It was empty: the other offices hadn't finished yet, plus it was January, so the thirty refugees from MacKenzie & Grierson had no problem getting served. A couple of the middle managers flashed company credit cards and the drinks racked up. By 6pm we were all pretty smashed: an otherworldly feeling, early Wednesday evening, and the entire office out drinking like it was the last day on earth.

I was getting a refill when the Norwegian Temp appeared next to me at the bar. She'd caused a stir among the office males since starting a couple of weeks before. She nudged me and said hello, and I made some awful comment about also having Viking blood. She laughed. I bought her a bloody mary.

We ate chips with mayonnaise and watched the chaos at the long table where most of our colleagues had congregated. Gavin from Finance was already asleep, and someone had put a chip up his nose. Others were dancing, or talking too close to each other. The Norwegian Temp – I'd been desperately listening to her conversation in the hope that she'd namecheck herself, because I had no idea what her name was – talked to me about her impressions of Scotland and touched my arm when I made her laugh. I remember taking a mouthful of fresh lager and seeing the light in her eyes and thinking: *wow, she wants to bang me*. My confidence had been shot to pieces by the Kathleen break-up so this was a major surprise.

More booze, and just when an argument broke out at the long table between two colleagues who'd been having a not-so-secret affair, the Norwegian Temp leaned her thigh against mine. I decided I was ready for this; ready to make the break from the Kathleen years. We left the pub hand-in-hand in front of colleagues too pished to notice.

We took a taxi to her place, a short ride up to Marchmont, not far from where Kathleen and I once shared a flat. Her flatmate was cooking chicken soup and we ate some together. I remember staring into the bowl at the wormy noodles and shreds of chicken and coriander leaves, wondering if my opportunity was slipping away. The girls talked about their uni courses and then suddenly the flatmate was gone and the Norwegian Temp was astride me.

In the bedroom I wrangled her clothes off and pulled my trousers down, and we found ourselves in an awkward grapple, her on all fours and me pushing my cock between her thighs. She laughed and flipped over. I struggled on top of her minus condom and slid inside her. She liked it, clutching my arse and pulling me in.

But then something weird happened.

My face pressed into her neck, I smelled her perfume properly for the first time. It was a pleasant smell – a smell almost like cinnamon. But it was totally different to Kathleen's perfume. For some reason it derailed me, and suddenly I felt like I wasn't in my body, like I wasn't Fin McPhail but somebody else. And I had this sense of myself as this hollow shell, in the hollow shell of the building, in a city empty of meaning.

I lost my erection. She asked me what was wrong, and when I said nothing she started to cry. As I laced up my shoes I remembered MacKenzie's speech earlier that day.

Kathleen was gone.

Amsterdam was calling.

[tape ends]

The Sunnyside Hotel

The tempo of the rain in Amsterdam is tidal – ebb and flow, sweep and fade, an overspill of the North Sea. Water drips off my nose as I move along the pavement towards the red-light district, retracing our steps from last night. Grey sheets of water unfold from the skies, cars whip through puddles, and wobbling cyclists try to guide their bikes and hold umbrellas at the same time. As I reach Damrak I catch a glimpse of a familiar slouch on the other side of the road: McKirdy, walking along with his hands embedded into the pockets of his hoodie. Despite the rain, his hood remains down.

I jog over the road, attracting an angry honk from a speeding taxi.

"McKirdy!"

He looks up. At first there is zero recognition on his face – a cold sore erupting on his lower lip – but then he nods, almost imperceptibly. "I'm lost, min. Cannae find ma hotel." He sways on his feet, blinks hard and shudders.

"You stoned?"

He shakes his head. "Aw kinds eh stuff. Started when we got back tae the hotel. We took the battery oot the smoke alarm, had a wee toke n got stuck intae the rest eh the 10p mix. Drank some Cloudburn. Me n Gilly. Razor fell asleep."

"Gilly was with you?"

"Aye, he came back wi us. Kipped on the floor. We must eh fallen asleep around four n I woke up at six absolutely fuckin *flyin*, man. *Flyin*. Had a shower but got freaked oot by the water jets, ken. Looked like needles drillin intae me. So I got ma gear on n headed oot for a walk. Walked for fuckin miles. Ended up in this massive park. I was seein hings, wee people movin in the bushes, stickin their heids oot, shoutin at me fae the trees. I pulled ma hood over ma heid n fell asleep on a bench." McKirdy fidgets. "Can we go tae the hotel? I've got the horrors bigtime."

The rain slackens as we make our way back out to Damrak and within five minutes we're outside Sunnyside Hotel. I've heard about these hotels but never been inside one – fleapits run by the immigrant community for budget travellers, rooms intended only for intoxicated sleep and luggage storage.

The receptionist is a middle eastern man with a brush-like moustache. He nods at us, and as we walk through the dimly lit corridors and up a set of carpeted stairs I get a flashback to Strange Fruit. McKirdy gives me his key and asks me to open the door.

Razor stands in the middle of the room, slapping moisturiser onto his bald head, wearing nothing except for a pair of Homer Simpson boxer shorts. His heavily tattooed chest and arms make him look like a Pictish warrior. "Look whit the cat dragged in," he says.

My eyes adjust to the gloom. Proof of last night's chaos is scattered all around: the torn open 10p Mix bag, dismantled smoke alarm surrounded by fronds of spilled tobacco, a half-empty bottle of Cloudburn 13 Year Old, an abandoned kebab, its innards congealed in white fat, a blanket tangled on the floor where Gilly presumably slept. Elsewhere, further evidence of the inhabitants' ethnic origin: a disjointed *Daily Record* open on the table, its font disturbingly familiar to my emigrant's eye; a six-pack of Irn-Bru peeking from a Samsonite suitcase, along with macaroon bars, Celtic shirt and kilt accessories.

Razor pulls a t-shirt on. "Look at the state eh ye, Stevie."

McKirdy bundles forward onto his bed. "Fuck min, I still need tae buy yon fuckin fridge magnet."

He's asleep in seconds.

"Fuckin nutter," says Razor, recapping his moisturiser. "See last night, wee man was hammered. I caught him in the pub bogs tryin tae tak a pish intae an airblade. Nearly blew his tadge aff."

I point at the macaroon bars. "Can I have one?"

"Aye, min. Fill yir boots."

I unwrap the macaroon and munch into it, scattering coconut shreds on the floor. I feel suddenly tired and sit down on the edge of McKirdy's bed. I stare at the cigarette-burned carpet and imagine what Ailsa is doing right now – playing with Wee Calvin maybe, or going through the seating arrangements with Mum for the wedding dinner. It's hard to fathom that in one week's time I am expected to be dressed in a kilt and watch my sister walk down the aisle. I pop open a can of Irn-Bru in the hope that its sugar-caffeine mix will give me a lift.

"How ye feelin?" says Razor.

"Pretty shite."

Razor sprays Lynx under his t-shirt, caps the aerosol and sighs. "Fucked up night, if ye ask me. It was on the cards. Gilly n Dingo have been nippin each other's heids for weeks."

"Dingo's missing. I woke up this morning and he's gone."

"Walkin it off. He's a walker. Mind his poem last night? While I was yomping through Fairy Glen..."

"What Gilly said about him and Ailsa. Is it true?" My voice cracks and Razor notices. He blinks in thought for a few seconds. Deciding whether to tell the truth or not? Will the omerta of drinking cronies prevail?

"I dinnae ken, that's the God's honest truth."

"Did Gilly say anything this morning?"

Razor shrugs. "He was gone when I woke up. Left a note." He hands me a porno card – three of Diamonds – showing a double penetration.

"On the back."

I turn it over. Scrawled in blue biro:

Gone for brekkie and BJ
Gilly

Razor slides a hand down his boxers and guddles his genitals thoughtfully. "Listen Fin, I dinnae agree wi the way Gilly operates wi lassies. See, I have a theory that ye can divide men intae three groups – lovers, shaggers n nerds. Dingo n McKirdy are lovers – they tend tae stick tae the wan lass, get aw mushy n that. You?" He holds a hand up apologetically. "Either a lover or a nerd, I dinnae ken ye well enough tae say. But I'm a shagger n so's Gilly. I go for lassies that are also shaggers – the yins that are intae it, can cope wi it mentally. Ken whit I mean?"

"I think so."

"For example, ye mind eh Morag Skelly at the distillery?"

I make a noise.

"I pumped her for a few months last year. She's in her late fifties but still game. It's a fair transaction – I like tae shag aw sorts eh women for purposes eh variety, she likes young cock. See?"

I make another noise.

"Now Gilly, he seems tae get a kick ootae pickin women that are *vulnerable*, ken? Single mums, junkies, women wi self-esteem issues."

"What you trying to say?"

Razor raises a hand to pacify me. "Dinnae get me wrong. Ailsa's a star. But we're aw human, right? Gilly's a better lookin laddie than Dingo. N Dingo gets on these right downers, ken?"

"So you think it's true?"

"I rule nothin oot, that's aw I'm sayin."

"Christ. Some friends, you lot. He's supposed to have fun this weekend? And you pricks rubbish his poetry, rip the pish out him..."

Razor's voice is quiet. "I'm a realist, Fin. I keep ootae folk's business n dinnae judge others. Dingo's ma mate – I'd kill for him. We have a great laugh at work, n doon at the Clachan quiz every Tuesday. If ye get involved in awbody's lives then yill have nae friends tae speak of. Cloudburn's a small toon. Ye ken that Fin, that's why ye left."

Behind me, a rattling snore from McKirdy.

"N see him," says Razor, nodding at the comatose form of Wee Stevie McKirdy. "He's the gentlest fucker ye could ever meet."

"And if what Gilly said is true? Where do your loyalties lie?"

"Rule number one: always stay awa fae yir mate's girl. If it's true, Gilly's fishfood tae me."

This answer satisfies me. Maybe it's the Irn-Bru-macaroon combination, but I'm buzzing, hyper-aware.

Razor tugs on his jeans and wedges his feet into croc-skin cowboy boots. "Dingo'll turn up. Gilly was probably talkin oot his erse. Tryin tae rile him, ken?" He pockets his wallet and scoops up a shrapnel of coins. "One solution, Fin – ye need a distraction. I'm planning tae visit a tattoo place – *emporium*, tae use McKirdy's favourite word – n could use yir help findin the fuckin place."

He hands me a Google Maps print-out: folded badly and stained with what I hope is orange juice. I know the street: not far from Rembrandtplein, about a fifteen minute walk.

Razor puts his jacket on – *a jacket* – and drapes his duvet over McKirdy, who coories under it unconsciously. It's an act of such simple tenderness that it blurs my eyes. An epic hangover, a macaroon bar and an Irn-Bru clearly transform me into a sentimental liability. We leave the hotel and head out in silence, and after two minutes reach the junction with Dam Square. Tourists and pigeons mingle on the cobbled expanse.

"So what tattoo you getting?"

This re-animates Razor. "Hmm. See, I'm thinkin eh two things. Option one, a Celtic band roond ma ankle. Standard stuff. Option two, n I dinnae ken if thull be able tae dae it..."

He hands me a piece of paper. It's a blown-up image of the Cloudburn fairy. Evil, bulbous-eyed wee fucker. I never told anyone, but I ripped it off from Alasdair Gray. Gave a copy of *Lanark* to the design agency and told them to replicate the look. After the launch I got a call from some Mancunian claiming to represent Gray's interests. I couriered a case of Cloudburn 18 Year Old to Mr Gray and never heard another peep.

We cross Dam Square, past the stadhuis where a bagpiper busks in full Highland regalia. Razor dumps half his shrapnel in the guy's case. Pigeons scatter.

Down Rokin, past the ripped up road where they're building the new metro line. It starts raining again and Razor produces a charcoal-coloured beanie. "See when yir a baldie? The cauld fuckin knifes right intae yir heid."

Muntplein clocktower, and past the cinema. I ask Razor if he fancies a beer for some Dutch courage.

"Good yin. Dutch courage."

Cafe de Vijzel. Heavy rock heaven. Pool tables upstairs, and full-on rock bar at ground level. We sit at a table with a candle melted into a wine bottle and drink a pint each. Sweet Home Alabama. Motorcycle Emptiness. Territorial Pissings. I enjoy forgetting everything. Razor shows me all his tattooes – the easily accessible ones, anyway – Aztec design on his left bicep, Hen Broon on his right bicep, a slightly scary reproduction of his two kids' faces over his heart. He drains his pint and nods at me. "Right. Whit's the plan for later?"

This throws me. It hadn't occurred to me that the stag party was ongoing. "The Nova Scotia?"

"Right ye are." We say our farewells, and he leaves me at a pedestrian crossing.

As I wait for the green man, my optimism fades. If it's true about Gilly and Ailsa, or even it isn't but Dingo believes it, then what does that mean for the wedding next week? I walk up Regulierdwarsstraat, past the restaurants and gay bars, and reach the crowded bottleneck of Leidsestraat, where trams, cars, bikes and pedestrians jostle for supremacy. I need to de-stress. Beer? Sleep? What do I need?

Your therapist told me exactly what you need.

Remembering Zasha's words stops me in my tracks. Did Eva tell Zasha to attack me?

I cross the road in the direction of Keizersgracht. Eva will surely be where she normally is on a Saturday afternoon: in bed. At least I can solve one mystery in the next hour.

It takes ten minutes to walk to her apartment. I climb the steps to the red door and press the buzzer. It can take as long as two minutes for her to get to the door if she's at the other end of her warehouse penthouse, so I lean in close to the intercom, away from the drizzle, and wait. And wait. I press the buzzer again, this time letting my thumb linger a few seconds more. She's probably sleeping off last night's clubbing. I try one more time then step back out into the street, wander over to the edge of the canal and peer up at the row of darkened windows.

My Irn-Bru and Macaroon induced happiness has faded to black, and now that I'm wet, cold, and alone, the paranoia creeps back. As I cross a bridge over towards Prinsengracht I notice a crowd up ahead, and a police van. Getting closer, I see the crowd gaze down at the canal, where two frogmen bob in the brown murk. One of the divers ducks under the surface, reappears, points below, removes his mouthpiece and says something to his partner.

Are they looking for a body?

An image of drowned Dingo flashes into my head and I walk faster, feet pounding the uneven cobbles, accelerating in the direction of The Nova Scotia.

Erotic Encounter No.304: Beermat Bingo

[noise of beer can opening]

A couple of months after the Norwegian temp incident, I moved to Amsterdam and was celibate for nine months or so. I would probably have stayed celibate, but you persuaded me out of retirement, Eva.

I still remember the buzz I got from that first email.

There I was, sitting at work, still thrilled after your appearance in the Nova Scotia, the favour you did for me. The way you sauntered into the pub in that mini-skirt and kissed me in front of Morrow and MacBean, their jaws practically hitting the floor. Revenge. The way we walked out of the pub arm-in-arm onto Prinsengracht, you clicking along on your heels with that tango dancer's strut. The light fading, the faint glimmer of the Westerkerk's golden spire. The way you kissed me on the cheek, and after your lips touched my skin, with perfect timing you told me to expect an email and walked away. I stood in the road and watched until you disappeared from sight. I nearly got run down by a taxi.

So there I was, at my desk, and when your email appeared I was like a teenager again. After two years of numbness it was like time travel, that feeling. Going back to a time when I felt things, and further back to 1991 and that first summer at the distillery, that woozy electricity in my guts every time I saw Kathleen. I was trembling when I double-clicked your email open. After I read it I printed it and sneaked outside to sit on a bench and read it again in the summer sunshine.

You told me to meet you in O'Reilly's, where my rebirth would begin.

I'm not a fan of O'Reilly's. There's only one authentic Irish pub in Amsterdam and O'Reilly's isn't it. The night I met you was a Wednesday, on the cusp of the weekly invasion of city break tourists. There was Champions League football on the big screen – the red shirts of Arsenal galloping across the turf, and some Londoners yelling them on like racehorses.

Just one beer, you told me. *You need to be on form.*

I asked you what you'd got planned for me. You just smiled. We drank our beers quickly and left. Out of the pub we turned right, and as we walked over to Dam Square, I realised we were going to the red-light district.

It was a clear night. The district was full of wandering single men, a smell of alcohol breath and budget aftershave and cigar smoke. You led me through the alleyways to a bar called The Sailor, always rowdy no matter the day of the week.

This is definitely your last beer, you told me. Then a line that had me reeling. *You've never been with a prostitute before, am I correct?*

I told you there was no way I would do it.

You said you knew the right people. *Professionals. Not trafficked, not co-erced. Independent sexual entrepreneurs certified to work with sex therapists.*

I shook my head.

Trust me, you said.

But now my heart was beating fast: your smile was validating the forbidden.

You took out a pen and laid out three beermats and flipped them over to reveal their white undersides. On the first you wrote VAGINAL. On the second, ORAL. The third: ANAL.

You flipped the beermats back, Heineken side up, and slid them around the table in intercrossing circles. You picked them up and shuffled them, returned them to the table, and slid them around again for good measure.

Pick one, you told me.

I went for the beermat on the right and tapped it once. You turned it over. VAGINAL.

You pointed out the window to where a constellation of red striplights glowed in the night. *I already chose someone*, you told me.

I finished my beer and we headed outside to find the *someone*. To be honest, I had no idea what to expect. We were only a few metres out the pub when you stopped and nodded to the window up the flight of stairs.

She sat on a high stool, long legs crossed and tilted sideways to accentuate her curves. She was beautiful, one of those Amsterdam conundrums where you just think *why the fuck is she here doing this*? Tumbledown brown curls, the cheekbones and eyes of a Czech supermodel. She could have used those looks for anything.

She smiled to reveal perfect teeth. You grabbed my hand and led me up the short flight of stairs, and the girl was already standing up, smoothing her bikini bottoms, tossing her hair back. She opened the door just as we reached it.

With a big smile on her face she said *Eva! Hey!*

You produced a crumpled fifty and said *Regular*.

I stepped through the gap into a small room that smelled of herbal candles. You were still speaking to the girl at the door as if you'd just dropped your kid off at the creche. Then the door clicked shut and it was just me and the girl.

What was her name again? Weird, that – I can remember all the details, like she was from Belarus, the light switch had a dimmer, she had one nipple pierced with a golden bolt, and when she laughed or gasped I could see her fillings – but I can't remember her name. Fucked up, eh?

It was quite quick in the end. I went to the bathroom to wash, and when I returned she was already naked and performing some kind of stretching exercise on the bed, legs asplay. She undressed me. I was trying not to think about the Norwegian Temp, about that moment when the cinnamon perfume derailed me. But stage one was negotiated successfully: I was naked, lying next to her on the narrow bed, and hard. Then the doubts started to flicker in my head. What if this doesn't work and I'm left with a Belarussian stranger consoling me, sex life in ruins?

But she was a professional, I have to say. It was almost like she sensed my worries. Her hand closed on my dick and what I thought was a caress was actually her putting the condom on. She rubbed her nipples against my chest and then sat over me. The doubts had gone. She slid me inside and bounced on me, buttocks slapping my thighs. She kept saying *come baby come.* It only took me a minute to do as instructed. At the moment of climax I looked towards the red curtain and noticed that it hadn't been drawn the full way across the window, and in fact, there was a narrow slice of exposed window, and you were standing there, Eva, face close to the glass, watching as I grabbed the Belarussian's haunches. When I looked back again you'd gone.

It's not just therapy, is it Eva? I'm starting to think you only want one thing out of this: to make me just as depraved as you.

[tape ends]

The Wish Tree

"Another pint?" says MacBean, lingering by the till.

I look down at my empty glass. "Aye. Go on then."

MacBean yanks the pump. Spit. Scoosh. Flow. The eighty shilling trundles into a fresh glass, its dark red yeastiness spooling round and round into a spinning froth. I watch, entranced.

"Where's your Cloudburn clowns?" he says, frowning down into the newborn pint.

"Hmmmph." I pick up a beermat and stab it against the bartop. "AWOL."

Gracefully he places the new pint onto the bar. "You want any grease to soak it up with?"

"You still doing breakfasts?"

"I'm willing to negotiate."

I take a few seconds to admire the fresh pint. Its unspoilt ruby redness satisfies me, pushes away the encroaching bleakness. "Ach, MacBean. I'm your best customer. Make me a full Scottish. Go on. Ten euros I'll pay you."

"That pish is your sales talk?" he says. "No wonder Cloudburn whisky is going down the tubes. How do you want your eggs?"

"Fried."

He gives me a solemn thumbs-up and disappears through the swing door.

It's strangely comforting to be alone in The Nova Scotia, perhaps because I'm safe here. The fruit machine flashes in the corner, promising treasure. Antlers dangle above. Tartan everywhere. Frank McAvennie grins over from the far wall. I reach out and touch my pint glass, still warm from the dishwasher, and lift its smooth promise to my lips.

In front of me is my scrap of paper. Four hours and four pints have not improved my list. A mouthful of eighty rinses away my delusions and I look at it again with my doubts confirmed:

New campaign based on name - flaming clouds, fiery skies?

Minimalist Scottish Zen - lower case brand name, samurai swords, ninja stars, oriental tartan fusion label

Something based on clouds - cirrus, cumulus, all the other names? (check Wikipedia)

Aim marketing at younger demographic - hip-hop, skateboarder, Cloudburn name in those bubble graffiti letters

Da Vinci code type bullshit - secret codes on the label, competitions with answers encrypted on website or at distillery.
Tartan. Definitely something tartan. Label looks like a kilt?

I pick up my pen and add a new bulletpoint:

I am fucked

I take a mouthful of pint.

I need a miracle. Something like what happened to Sproat's Botanical. It's a famous story in the industry: a boutique Scottish gin, popular in style bars, but low-selling and struggling against the big names. And then, from nowhere, a gangsta rapper decides that he likes the gin so much he's going to dance around with a bottle in his hand during his latest video while rapping the refrain over a scuzzy backbeat: *Like a Tyrannosaurus I'm tyrannical, gettin loose on Sproat's Botanical.* Cue a 600% spike in sales. I worked alongside the Sproat's marketing manager at the time, a cheeky bastard from Croy called Dermot McGooley. Within a month he was flying to LA and wearing Armani. Last I heard he was one of the top bods at Bacardi.

I take another gulp of the pint. I'm going to lose my job next week: that's clear enough. My right hand begins to tremor. I watch it with horrified detachment, shaking so much that I can't grip the pint glass. My heart flutters: Dingo. Gone.

I imagine him in transit somewhere, on his way to a new life. On a train crossing Germany. At Schiphol waiting for the New York flight. I press the tip of the biro hard onto the paper, gouging a pinpoint hole. Rain batters the window, and I peer down into my pint. I know what I must do, more than anything this weekend. My career is already goosed. What I must do is look after my sister.

Five minutes after wolfing my all-day breakfast I'm walking head down through the smirr, saying a silent prayer. *Please let the light be on. Please*. If the light is on then Dingo is home. If the light is on then at least he's alive and still in the country, and we can deal with all the other stuff in due course. I tilt my head up into the glare of the streetlights and look at the apartment windows as I turn the corner onto Lindenstraat.

The light in my living-room is on.

I break into a jog, open my door, and scramble up the stairs. "Dingo! Dingo!"

The living-room is empty. "Dingo!"

Then I notice what's on the oak table.

My mobile phone.

My fucking mobile phone.

Next to it, a scrawled note –

CALL 06 2529 0723

Goose-pimples on my skin. I key in the number. A purr and click down the line, and the call connects.

"So," says a voice. "Findlay McPhail I presume?"

My throat is dry. "Yeah."

"Do you want to see your friend again?" The voice is Dutch, tinged with American.

"Fuck."

"I'll take that as a yes."

"Where is he?"

"Here. At Strange Fruit."

"Strange Fruit?"

"Don't pretend to be surprised. We thought he was you. He was so stoned he couldn't speak. We let him sleep it off for a few hours. And now he's speaking. And he's not you."

"No. He's not me."

"He told me something interesting. About an old bottle of whisky worth fifty thousand pounds. The Bottle of Brotherhood?"

"I'm going to call the police."

"Yes, and if you do that, I release your friend out the back door as soon as they turn up, and Zasha tells the police all about the violent assault on Thursday night. Oh, and I've got your mother's telephone number, remember. And CCTV footage."

My head hurts. I press my fingers into my scalp.

"So," says the man. "Here's the deal. You bring the whisky to Strange Fruit, along with two thousand euros to compensate me for lost business. You bring this to Strange Fruit and we don't hurt your friend. You've got until ten o'clock and then we start breaking his teeth. Or his fingers, whichever he values more."

He hangs up.

I sit down and slump over the table. I'm just glad I have the anaesthetic of five pints swilling in my blood. Oh Dingo. Why didn't you go to Dublin for your stag? Or Blackpool? Or the Cloudburn Miners Club?

My mobile rings, vibrating the table, tremoring into my cheek and through my teeth.

The phone display shows the one name I don't want to see. Ailsa.

I move to switch it off, but stop myself. What if she's been calling Dingo as well and getting no response?

"Ailsa?"

"At last! What's wi the radio silence? I've been phonin aw day!"

"Well, it's a stag, Ailsa. You know what it's like."

"Where's Dingo? He's never answered any eh ma calls or texts."

"Aye, he's a wee bit under the influence right now. Ate some spacecake, just sleeping it off."

"Christ, Fin. I thought ye were going to keep an eye on him."

"I am. Ailsa, I promised you. He's behaving himself, drinking plenty of beer, occasional joint, but nothing to worry about. How are you?"

"Oh just fine, brother of mine."

"Sis, don't worry, OK?"

Silence.

She sighs. "OK. I'll stop worryin. But tell him to call me in the mornin, right?"

Two thousand euros, and the Bottle of Brotherhood. "Aye. Take care Ailsa."

I go to the toilet. Breathe in, breathe out. Beery pish trundling into the pan. Flush. Through the porthole window I see my neighbour eating dinner with a heavy-set woman, both laughing, glasses of red wine on the table. He glances over, and I nod at him. He smiles and raises his glass. It's nice that someone's weekend is going well.

Back downstairs, the flat eerily silent. I sit on the sofa and look down at the floor. The only thing I've ever stolen was a handful of jelly sweets from Mitchell's 10p Mix tray. I think about the Bottle of Brotherhood and its faded labels: a piece of Cloudburn's history. And then I think about some quick-witted distillery manager in the 1950s asking one of the coopers to decant spirit into an old bottle. The first fib of many. The same distillery manager commissioning a skilled forger to fashion ancient labels and scuff the bottle up, make it look fifty years older than it actually was. A poster campaign, a bit of spin, and there you go: a legend created from thin air.

Maybe it's time to bury the legend.

I grab my bike keys off the bookshelf and do some quick mental arithmetic. Twenty minutes to cycle to work, twenty minutes in-and-out of the office, twenty minutes to Strange Fruit. I should make it for around nine thirty. I actually feel happy for a moment. I'm going to lose my job anyway, so fuck it. Fuck Newt. It's better that a psycho-pimp gets the Bottle of Brotherhood than Newt Sarkissian.

A brainwave comes to me – I rummage through my documents and yes, there it is – the blank passcard the

Lithuanian temp used a few months back. If it still works I can get into work incognito. To be on the safe side I grab a pair of gloves as well: better not to leave any fingerprints around the immediate scene of the crime. I pour a snifter of Cloudburn 1978 for luck and knock it back in one.

It's spitting outside. I kick off on my bike and pedal through the empty streets, past cafes tightly packed with Saturday night crowds. They'll be drinking their *biertjes* and wines and snacking on deep-fried cheese and processed meat, oblivious to the idiot on the bike outside, the numpty off to steal a bottle of whisky from his work in order to save his future brother-in-law. I cycle over the bridge and up onto Haarlemmerstraat. The wind picks up and I pump the pedals faster.

Sloterdijk is desolate: windy, damp, abandoned pet rabbits hopping around in the undergrowth. The office blocks are dark, save for the occasional square of light in the grids of black windows. I bike to the back of the Stalwart building and try the temp passcard to access the basement car park – it bleeps and the door unclicks. The office closes at midnight: the company is thoughtful enough to allow access to those who wish to work late at the weekends. The security guard has possibly seen me on CCTV but in my experience of weekend work, security's attention will be on online poker.

I lock my bike up in the cage and take the fire stairs. It's a long climb up to the eighth floor but I can't risk the lift. On the way up I stop at the fifth floor for a breather. I lean on the banister and think, for the first time, about how I'm going to steal the bottle. It's locked in the display cabinet, and the keys are on Newt's desk somewhere – just last week I saw him give them to Olly so he could replace the old Dostoevsky Vodka bottle with the new electric-blue, frosted glass version. The keys are hard to miss, as they're attached to a wooden tulip keyring. But what if I can't find the keys?

I climb the remaining floors, the booze wearing off. I wave my pass in front of the sensor and a loud bleep unlocks the door. I open it to be confronted with darkness – sweet, empty darkness – and fumble against the wall for the light switch. The overhead lights judder, blink twice, and flood the department with sterile white light. My eyes adjust, heartbeat returning to normal. I can do this. I know I can do this.

Newt's desk is cluttered with dirty coffee cups and printouts filed in green and red plastic folders. The closest his desk comes to having a personal touch is an LA Lakers pennant dangling next to a list of phone numbers. Where would he keep the keys? I open the drawers and rifle through layers of crap: chocolate bar wrappers, chewed pens, a squidgy stress reliever in the shape of a breast, batteries, an empty pack of condoms, and loose staples.

Underneath the desk is a huge package, a cardboard box mummified in shrink-wrap, the address stuck to the front with masking tape. Next to this is a green sportsbag. His PC, the keyboard dirty from spilt coffee, and behind the monitor, nothing. Trays full of correspondence and printed Powerpoint presentations; I flick through the sheaves of paper hoping for a suspicious bulge, but again, no result. I lean back on his chair, letting the suspension bounce me up again.

Behind Newt's monitor I notice last year's Inca Tequila gift carton – a pastel red and purple monstrosity, with yellow lizards wriggling around the text. I reach out and pick it up and something metallic rattles. I peel off the plastic lid, tip the carton towards my hand, and out slide the keys: heavy in my palm, entangled, the wooden tulip keyring chipped and splintered.

"Ya beauty."

I move quickly, first to my desk where I collect a spare bottle of Cloudburn as a decoy. I put my gloves on, and really start to feel like a criminal. There are six or seven keys and I sort through them until I find two that look small enough to fit the lock, try the first and get it right first time. The lock clicks open smoothly, and I ease the glass door back on its hinges. The Bottle of Brotherhood is tucked in the back corner, and I have to remove three bottles of Sproat's Botanical in order to reach it safely. My fingers close on its cold, narrow neck and I lift it up and out, and place it gently down on the carpeted floor. It's the first time I've touched this bottle in over five years. A different world, a world in which I was married and buoyant with hope. I take the decoy bottle of Cloudburn and place it in the back corner, careful to rotate the bottle so the label is at the same angle. If anyone knows the display well enough they'll see instantly that this is a different bottle – the bottles and labels are different colours, and different designs, but I have a gut feeling that nobody will notice.

At least for a few weeks, by which time I'll be long gone. I replace the bottles of Sproat's, lock the cabinet, and return to my desk with the Bottle of Brotherhood.

At this moment, I realise a basic error: I've brought nothing to carry the bottle in. I should have brought a bag and some bubble wrap, or at least a sweater for protective padding. There must be a plastic bag somewhere in the department, and bubblewrap for all the packages we send out. Some string too, so I can tie it to my bike.

I've just placed the bottle gently down on my desk and taken two steps towards the cupboard when I hear a noise that flash-freezes my blood. The lift pinging.

I move fast, sprint across to the far wall and turn off the lights. Turn and sprint back the way through the shadowy gloom, just as the lift doors rumble open and somebody coughs. Whoever is getting out the lift is only half a metre from the light switch. I fling myself towards the nearest hiding place, which happens to be behind the Wish Tree.

Light re-floods the department. I shuffle up close to the chipboard bulk of the Wish Tree. I've never been this close to it before. It was Stalwart's attempt to give something back to the community, to display our outstanding corporate citizenship. The company linked up with a local home for adults with learning difficulties and pledged to make their dreams come true. Their wishes dangle from the branches around me: *I WANT TO SWIM WITH DOLPHINS. I WANT TO EAT 5 BURGERS AT McDONALD'S. I WANT TO MEET*

PATRICK KLUIVERT. To my knowledge, the McDonald's wish was the only one fulfilled.

The new arrival coughs again, and something about that phlegmy growl makes me grimace.

Newt.

I hear the Microsoft jingle as a PC boots up. A tearing noise, the squeak of plastic wrapping unravelling, carboard being torn apart. The package under his desk? The clunk of heavy objects placed on wood, drawers opening and closing. An awkward silence, and for a moment, I think that Newt – if it is Newt – has noticed something wrong, something different about his desk; but then he starts humming Thin Lizzy's *The Boys are Back in Town*, and I know for sure it's him. Keyboard rattling, which means he has his back to me. I step across to the edge of the Wish Tree and peek between the crepe paper leaves.

Newt's wearing a white sweatshirt and white jeans. At his feet sits the package, polystyrene chips and shrinkwrap scattered on the carpet tiles. He's holding something in his hand – a bottle – with more lined up on his desk. He places the bottle next to his keyboard and delves back into the box, this time coming up with a folder. He takes sheets of paper out and spreads them across the desk like oversized playing cards. He laughs.

A ringtone, Dire Straits' *Money for Nothing*.

He fumbles in his pocket and stands up. *Please Newt you fucking twat – do what you usually do*. He mutters into the mobile and starts walking in the direction of the corridor. *Keep going, you fuck*. He keeps going. My colleagues refer to this habit as his lap of honour – when he receives a call he walks out into the corridor, round by the break-out area and toilets, then back into the department through the parallel corridor, talking loudly all the time, a peacock strut to remind us who's boss. I watch him recede down the corridor. This is my moment.

Moving swiftly, I retrieve the Bottle of Brotherhood from my desk, pause until I'm certain Newt's voice is far away, and move towards his desk. The green sportsbag. I can put the bottle in his forgotten green sportsbag and then, if I time it right, follow in his slipstream and just as he moves past the break-out area, make my exit down the fire stairs. Striding quickly, heart thumping, I make my move.

When I reach Newt's desk, I freeze.

The bottles he's lined up are both familiar and horribly alien. Mock-ups, as we call them in the trade, created by a design agency. And these bottles are mock-ups for a new design of Cloudburn.

Each bottle sports a different label and design, but what they all have in common is the name. *CLOUD NINE*. And underneath this, in flowing text, *COCKTAIL WHISKY*.

I'm already in shock: and then I notice the papers spread out on Newt's desk. Architect's plans, and artist's impressions of how the Cloudburn distillery will look following its conversion into the Cloud Nine Luxury Hotel Complex. The warehouse where I lost my virginity to be transformed into a fitness centre. The staff canteen where I met Kathleen to be converted into the hotel's reception area. A new building stretching out past the warehouse, meaning that the rest of Fairy Glen will be cleared. In the colourful diagrams, happy little people walk around the pebbled grounds, and there's even a family having a picnic on a grassy area that's currently the staff car park. A picnic, in Scotland?

My stomach flips. Newt's voice is getting close, maybe near the break-out area.

I move quickly: grab the sportsbag from under the desk, unzip it – revealing a mouldy towel, t-shirt, shorts, a pair of yellowing Y-fronts, *NEWT SARKISSIAN* stencilled on the bag's nylon lining in marker pen – and slide in the Bottle of Brotherhood, making sure it's swaddled with enough sweaty gear to protect it. Zip up the bag, sling it on my shoulder, and jog into the corridor.

Newt's voice is receding as I stride silently towards the fire door. If he notices the bag is missing straight away then I could be in trouble. But he won't notice. If fate is on my side tonight, he won't notice. I open the fire door and move swiftly down the stairs.

Erotic Encounter No.313: Candy Stripes & Balaclavas

[noise of beer can opening]

I'll be honest with you Eva. This latest encounter was seriously fucked up. I know it's supposed to expand my mind, but what the fuck?

I did as instructed and took part in your little treasure hunt. First of all went to Cafe Smalle and asked the barman if I could have a word with Hilbert. Turned out Hilbert was the barman. He gave me the envelope and poured a La Chouffe, said the lady had paid for it. I sat at the bar and read your note. You like your mysteries, eh? An address in Oud Zuid, an appointment for three o'clock and one instruction – *do what they tell you.*

I sat in the cafe with the beer and to be honest I thought about packing it in. Sitting listening to people chatting around me, reading their newspapers, drinking their hot chocolates laced with rum, their mint teas, eating their pea soup, sitting there in this beautiful old converted gin distillery, the trees green outside, the tinkle of bicycle bells, flavoured tobacco smoke wafting in through the cafe door. I got a bit emotional. I felt like

I wanted something different. Just to bike down to Muntplein instead, go to the Tuschinski to see a movie. Eat some popcorn, feel my feet stick to the antique red carpets. And afterwards, cycle through Vondelpark and get that childish feeling of freewheeling along, the breeze in my hair.

But then I realised I was getting a hard-on and was wearing soft cotton trousers so I had to leave the pub quick-smart. Ten minutes later I was wheeling to a stop outside an Oud Zuid townhouse. No nerves: just a readiness to perform. It was five to three: I pressed the doorbell.

The door opened a couple of inches. It was dark inside. A voice told me to go to the room on the left, take my clothes off, and put on the costume on the bed. I nudged open the door into a small bedroom. A large pile of shoes and clothes in one corner – like a wardrobe had been emptied on the floor – and on the bed, as promised, the costume. A pile of costumes in fact, all exactly the same.

Again I had that feeling of quitting. The costume wasn't complicated: a black balaclava, and striped leggings. The stripes were alternately candy-pink and white. I undressed and stood there, bollock-naked, looking at the leggings. I picked up the balaclava – I hadn't worn one since I was about seven years old, and this was the full-on IRA number with holes for the eyes and mouth. The leggings were soft to the touch. I put them on. A bit tight, they stopped just above my knees. I pulled the balaclava over my head and at that moment the door opened.

A tubby, hairy man, also wearing a balaclava and candy-striped leggings, with a stubby erection pointing at me. *Come join the fun*, he said.

The living-room had been converted for the occasion. Orgy makeover. Mattresses on the floor, scented candles, plastic glasses of champagne next to finger-bowls of blue pills – presumably not M&Ms – bunches of grapes draped here and there, like the host had assumed orgy catering was unchanged since the days of the Roman Empire. The ambience was spoiled somewhat by a multi-pack of kitchen roll next to the fireplace.

Maybe twenty people, all wearing the same balaclavas and leggings. It was all group stuff going on. A collapsed human pyramid in the middle of the room, limbs grappling for purchase, bodies plugged into each other messily. A gleaming foursome sipping post-fuck champagne. The tubby man wandered around with a hand-held camera, filming the proceedings. Tubby waved me over in the direction of the clusterfuck.

I did what was expected of me.

What I've been trained for.

I sneaked out. In the changing room I had a dizzy spell and sat on the bed for a bit. I biked through Vondelpark, breeze in my hair again, but still felt bleak inside. So I went to the Tuschinski, bought a jumbo popcorn and a bucket of cola and sat in a row on my own where nobody could see the tears running down my face.

We need to talk, Eva.

[tape ends]

Return to Strange Fruit

The night is calmer, wind muffled to a light breeze. I pedal slowly, not wanting to take any chances with the Bottle of Brotherhood. The sportsbag is tied to the rack above my back wheel with elastic straps and every time I stop at traffic lights I glance behind to check. As I pedal, what I saw on Newt's desk begins to sink in.

Cloudburn is light enough to mix well with other beverages, hard and soft, and with a bit of money behind a campaign for Cloud Nine cocktail whisky, could probably get a decent sales push in the U.S. But it would just be a fad, something that wouldn't last. A couple of years of short-term profit with no long-term future.

Second step: Stalwart uses all maturing stocks for Cloud Nine if it's selling, or alternatively, sells stocks to blenders (who have always valued Cloudburn's versatility in adding a delicate touch to the roughest blended scotch). Third step: whisky production stops at the distillery. And that'll be the end of whisky production in Cloudburn after around a hundred and twenty years. Get rid of the staff – Da, Dingo, Gilly, Razor, McKirdy and about thirty others – and announce the brand is no longer profitable, and with regret,

Stalwart Brands has been forced to mothball Cloudburn distillery. Of course, there might be an outcry, but dozens of Scottish distilleries were mothballed in the 80s and 90s and in this tough new corporate world, they will tell us, difficult decisions must be made. And with the staff and whisky gone all that will be left will be the distillery buildings and the substantial surrounding grounds.

Step three. Stalwart Brands, already with a sideline in hotels in the U.S., begins its new project. Work begins on converting the distillery into a luxury hotel. The diggers move in and tear up the rest of Fairy Glen. The well-constructed nineteenth century warehouse buildings provide the builders with solid foundations to create hundreds of guestrooms, with space for conference rooms, maybe a swimming pool, a couple of restaurants. Cheap, hard-working staff imported from the fringes of Europe. Give it two years and the Cloud Nine Luxury Hotel complex will be up and running. Just over an hour's drive from Edinburgh or Glasgow airports, beautiful views of the hills and surrounding countryside, Stirling a twenty minute drive away, and far enough away from the town of Cloudburn for guests to never have to see the concrete shopping plaza and the puke-stained pavements. Cloud Nine Hotel, ladies and gentlemen. Exclusive, five stars, created for society's finest. A worthy competitor for Gleneagles, a flagship venue for Stalwart Brands in Europe, and a fist in the face for my family and the town I grew up in.

At the top of Overtoom I spot an ATM window glowing in the night, and juggling my four cards, take out the requested two thousand euros. Trams clang and glide up and down the long narrow street. I untie the sportsbag from the back of the bike and walk the short distance to Strange Fruit.

Newt's bag smells of mildew and socks. I'm glad of the breeze, and give myself a few moments in the fresh air before finally pressing the Strange Fruit buzzer. When the intercom crackles I lean up to the plastic grille and tell it what it wants to hear.

"Findlay McPhail, here to see the proprietor."

The door buzzes and unlocks.

It's the same woman working on reception, the one with the candy floss hair and wet liver lipstick.

"Go downstairs," she says and motions to a frosted glass door.

I do as she says, walking slowly over the carpet with hexagonal patterns. Through the door: into a gloomy corridor, and down steep stairs, the carpet frayed and sprinkled with cigarette ash. At the bottom is an even darker corridor and I pause while my eyes adjust. At the other end is a door with the word *ZERO* written on the front in marker pen.

I'm halfway along the corridor, heart beating fast, when I hear movement behind me.

"Fucker," says a female voice.

It's Zasha, hobbling towards me. She's hunched, a bit like Quasimodo, and I realise at the last moment that this is because she's carrying a baseball bat, and in the process of swinging it at me.

I duck just in time. The bat crashes into the wall and showers plaster dust onto the carpet. She swipes it back the way but succeeds only in clunking me on the arm. I move backwards, arms outstretched, protecting the Bottle of Brotherhood. "I've got money for you! Compensation!"

She raises up the bat to shoulder height, ready to swing again, a smudge of purple bruising under her right eye.

The door opens behind me but I'm scared to turn my back on Zasha.

A voice. "Zasha, stop it. Let's settle this like civilised human beings."

Zasha lowers the bat.

I turn, slowly. The man standing in the doorway has a red goatee beard, scraggy ginger hair, and a scowl on him like he's just leapt off a longboat.

"The famous Findlay McPhail," he says. "Get in here now."

He steps to one side and jabs his thumb towards the room. As I pass through the narrow door he gives me a hard shove. The room is surprisingly large: a desk covered in graffiti, pot plants, a PC, a Buddha statuette, a flatscreen TV, a cabinet stocked with dozens of bottles of booze, and at one side, sitting in plastic chairs, two men.

"Employees of mine," says the redhead. They look almost exactly the same, buzzcut hair and bouncer's suits, except one is white and the other North African.

"Sit." Redhead points at a pouffe in the middle of the room.

I crouch down on the small leather stool and slide the sportsbag off my shoulder.

"Do you have what I asked for?"

"Where's Dingo?"

"Who?"

"My friend. The one you kidnapped."

"The stoner. You'll see him in a minute." Redhead clicks his fingers. "The whisky. The money."

I open the bag and unravel the dirty sports gear from around the Bottle of Brotherhood. I place the bottle on the carpet, open my wallet, take the cash out. When I move to stand up, the white bouncer speaks.

"Stay in your fucking seat."

I do as he says and lower my buttocks to the pouffe again. The brown bouncer comes over and takes the cash and the bottle. He transfers the ransom to Redhead, who sits on the desk watching me. I remove my gloves, crime finally completed.

"So this whisky is worth fifty thousand pounds?"

"That's the most recent valuation I'm aware of. But you could never sell it, unless you found a private collector willing to keep his mouth shut."

Redhead examines the bottle, turning it over in his hands, reading the label. "And you work for this distillery?"

"Yes, but probably not for much longer."

"Zasha!" Redhead beckons her over. He shuffles the cash and gives her a few notes.

"Billeeee… that's not fair."

"You get more compensation," says Billy. "But not with the bat."

Before I have time to digest what he's said, Zasha strides over and punches me in the face.

The momentum flips me off the pouffe and I fall backwards onto the carpet. She jumps on top of me, punching and clawing, and I huddle into a ball, shielding myself from her blows, her nails gouging at my hands, trying to get at my eyes. Then the next thing I know, the bouncers are dragging her out into the corridor.

"Fucker!" she yells.

Blood in my mouth, hands scratched to fuck. As I lie on the carpet, getting my breath back, Billy picks up Zasha's baseball bat. He walks slowly towards me. "Only one person in this establishment is permitted to use a baseball bat."

He swings it down hard and sharp and cracks me on the thigh.

"Ahhhhh fuck!"

He arcs it down again, this time catching me in the ribs. Blinding pain. I can't breathe, or move.

Billy sniffs, wipes a hand over his mouth. The two bouncers return, and Billy says something to them in Dutch. The bouncers hoist me to my feet, socket-twisting my arms. Billy slides open a desk drawer and lifts out an industrial stapler.

"We need to teach you a lesson," says Billy.

The white bouncer lurches downwards and grabs my legs, and brown bouncer pincers my arms apart. Before I realise what's happening they have me splayed in a starfish position on the carpet.

Billy unbuckles my belt. I writhe and wriggle. His calloused fingers hook into my waistband and yank my jeans and boxers down.

"Generally speaking, people with genital injuries rarely go to the police," he says. "Staples in your private area only mean one thing to doctors. Weird sex games."

I holler and scream. A sandpapery finger and thumb pinches my scrotum and stretches it upwards.

"You will pay me a tax," says Billy. "A thousand euros every month for one year. If you miss an instalment, then we're going to have some fun with this stapler."

He presses a thumb on my windpipe until blackness prickles behind my eyelids.

They release me, and I gulp for air.

"Get up you piece of shit. My friends here will come to visit you next week for the first payment."

I'm halfway through tugging my trousers back up when the bouncers scoop me up and frogmarch me out the room, stopping only to pull the door to Room Zero shut.

The brown bouncer throws me into the wall. I bounce and spin back to the floor. Carpet fibres in my mouth, the world darkening. A foot nudges me. "Here's your friend."

The thought of seeing Dingo revives me. I raise my head and squint through the gloom. The white bouncer leads a man down the corridor towards me. A man in a Distillery Boys t-shirt.

The hostage.

But not Dingo.

Gilly.

Suddenly the air is back in my lungs. "What the fuck?"

Gilly stares at me, eyes alive with fury, face bruised from Dingo's punch last night. I return his stare. "What the fuck are you doing here?"

Gilly wriggles against the bouncer's grip. "I could ask ye the same question."

"But how...?"

"Out!" yells the brown bouncer. He swings a steel-capped boot and catches me on the shin.

They push Gilly and me up the stairs. I watch Gilly's back as we tumble upwards.

White bouncer holds the door open and brown bouncer takes the time to push us each out onto the street individually. I slump onto the rain-drenched pavement and land on my battered thigh. The door slams shut behind us. It takes two attempts before I'm able to stand up, and I look up to see Gilly glowering at me. "Fuckin bastard."

He throws a punch, but a burst of adrenalin saves me: I dodge to the left just in time. His fist arcs past and I elbow him in the face. Bone on bone. He staggers back and with renewed anger thuds into me and we clatter to the pavement. Wet stone, the grit of a puddle in my face. Kick and wriggle: his knee thuds into the small of my back. Stink of sweat and piss off him. We break, get back to our feet.

"Ye fuckin two-faced bastard," he says, taking a moment to wipe the blood-smear from his mouth. "Think yir better than the rest eh us, but in that brothel ridin hoors."

"Prick. How the hell did you end up in Strange Fruit?"

Gilly spits at my feet. "I went oot for some breakfast. Wandered around for ages n just ma fuckin luck, I found masel ootside yir flat. Still had the keys on me, decided tae get ma bag. But I was so fuckin monged I couldnae get up the stairs n when I came back out yon cunt grabbed me."

I look him in the eyes. The Big Question. "What you said last night about Ailsa and Wee Calvin. Is it true?"

His expression changes. Do I see regret? My arms flop to my side. Energy gone.

He yells at me. "Naw. But I have fucked yir sister. Ewan Semple's party?" When he sees my face he smiles. "That's right. The famous Gang Bang Gang..."

Blowtorch fury. I whirl into him, and everything else disappears – Amsterdam, the night sky, Dingo, Ailsa, Wee Calvin – just me and this ancient rage.

He parries my fists and breaks away.

"I was number two. Sloppy seconds. But at least I wasnae number five."

I swing for him and miss, hear him laugh: dizzy, I fall to the ground. He kicks me – once, twice – and the third time I grab his leg and yank him sideways. His head thunks on the pavement and he grunts. Back on my feet, and he lies on the ground like a dying wasp, arms and legs quivering, moving against the ground for purchase. The idea rushes towards me: jump on him. Jump on his head.

But something – someone – slams into me.

Five guys, early twenties, spiky hair and skinny jeans.

At first they yell and plead in Dutch but when Gilly tells them to *git tae fuck* they click that they're dealing with non-indigenous conflict.

"Guys, you need to cool it!"

"Easy, easy…"

"You gonna stop this fight now?"

While their attention is on Gilly I walk away. Stumbling at first, as my momentum picks up I get into a stride, breathing regulating, adrenalin still fizzing inside.

A shout comes from behind me. "Stay off the alcohol, you crazy Brit!"

I hear Gilly's voice, confused. "Leave me alone ya Dutch cunts!"

I walk on, past my bike, too shaky to ride it right now. At the top of the Overtoom the green man pip-pips and I continue over the road, towards the lights shining through the trees, in the direction of Leidseplein, ribcage pulsing from where the baseball bat struck, head spinning. Gilly. Fucking Gilly. The swish of a taxi, wheels on wet tarmac. *I almost jumped on his head. With my boots, these fucking heavy boots.* Laughter from two passing cyclists. *I could have killed him.*

I should have killed him.

The American Hotel. Its bright lights and gurgling fountain stop me in my tracks. Through the condensation-misted windows of the hotel bar, the vague shape of drinkers – a red sweater, a white shirt – remind me of the real world. A world where police officers arrest those who jump on others' heads. A world where my sister nervously sits in front of the TV, worrying about her fiancé, worrying about the wedding, worrying about her young son's future. But probably not worrying about the Gang Bang Gang anymore.

I sit on the fountain wall. My cargo pants are torn: one pocket hangs off like a spaniel's ear. For the first time I notice that part of my front tooth is missing, and push my tongue against a sharp diagonal ridge. Other damage: bruised thigh, ribcage, a soreness on the side of my head, grated knuckles, and more of the familiar nipple pain. My exertions have torn the healing scab open.

A bleep next to the nipple shocks me, and it takes a moment before I realise it's my mobile. I reach into my jacket pocket. *1 message received.* From Morrow:

going to see eva's
show with Dingo.
You dirty amoeba!

On the Rocks

Rain slashing down, I walk close to the buildings and jog over the open streets. Despite the weather, Saturday night is in full swing: gangs of lads and girls kick their way down Leidsestraat, interrupted from their laughter only by the slow grind of the trams along the street, splitting the sea of people. I turn left onto Prinsengracht and leave the crowds behind. The sudden quiet is disturbing. I try calling Morrow again, but he's not picking up.

Eva's show? You dirty amoeba?

The last time I spoke to her she reassured me that my recent doubts were natural, a barrier I had to break through. I'm reminded of Kathleen, Hamish telling her that her pain and hurt were part of *her journey*. A necessary stage.

The Nova Scotia. I slick a hand back through my rain-sodden hair and push the door open. The familiar grind of metal on stone, the familiar smell of spilt beer and fried potato. As soon as I enter it's obvious Razor and McKirdy have annexed the pub: sitting at the window table, they're loud and leery, laughing and howling abuse at each other. I glance over at the bar. MacBean looks nervous, pouring another two pints.

I shake his hand.

"The clowns have returned."

"Aye, unfortunately."

"What happened to your face?"

"Got in a few scraps."

"Pint?" He points at a vacant beermat.

"No. Listen, was Morrow here?"

"Aye, he left half an hour ago. He took one of your clowns with him."

"Where was he going?"

MacBean looks at me, puzzled. "The exhibition. I thought you were already there?"

When he sees the blank look on my face he rummages around behind the bar and hands me a postcard.

Splashes and spurts of colour on the front. I turn it to the flipside and the shock makes me drop the postcard – it flutters to the floor.

MacBean sighs. "Morrow brought it in earlier. Are you sure you don't want a pint?"

I'm back out into the rainy night in seconds, jogging across the cobbles in the direction of Eva's apartment. As I cross the bridge onto the Keizersgracht I see the lights are on in her penthouse, and as I get closer, see people crowding close to the windows, glass steamed up. The door is wedged open and the distant chatter of a party drifts out. I climb the stairs to the top floor. The door is open, and on it a poster, the same design as the postcard.

THE SEXUAL AMOEBA

A MULTI-MEDIA ART EXHIBITION &
EXPLORATION OF RECLAIMED SEXUALITY
BY EVA ROSIE
322d KEIZERSGRACHT
8PM SATURDAY 3RD OCTOBER 2008

I slip into the crowded living-room, the tables and the kitchen worktop covered with trays of canapés and bottles and glasses. The guests are quite well-dressed: or at least what counts for well-dressed in the Netherlands. The men wear jeans and shirts with rumpled H&M-style suit jackets, the women skirts and lipstick and boots. It's busy enough for me to cross the room without being noticed. I knock back an unclaimed glass of champagne and continue to the far wall, where the door to Eva's office is wide open.

I walk on through.

A flatscreen TV shows the scratchy, black-and-white pictures of me at Strange Fruit. Tumbling onto the carpet with Zasha. Through the speakers, a male Scottish voice: "*...the sheen of bacon grease on the paper bag. I think about sex. Positioning myself behind Kathleen on the bed... her hand tucking me inside and banging hard into her, our thighs slapping.*"

Dizziness. A heat in my face like lava.

Ten, maybe twelve paintings, carefully mounted on the bare brick walls. It only takes a few seconds to register that the one thing these paintings have in common is me.

The painting nearest the door shows, in the unmistakable style of Edward Hopper, a brown-haired man standing at the end of an alleyway. Along the alleyway are rows of windows, each one lit by a burning red light, the women behind the windows are white, Asian, black: the man looks undeniably alone, his face blank of expression. The card on the wall reads *The Loneliness of the Alleyway*, EUR 500.

The next painting – *Innocence Lost*, EUR 400 – has the look of a feverish nightmare. It shows the same brown-haired man standing naked inside a darkened building made of large bricks. *Wait*: not bricks, cardboard boxes. The man stands opposite a naked woman – two white triangles cover her breasts, and one white triangle obscures her crotch – and it clicks that this is supposed to be me in the storeroom with Morag Skelly. Her expression is blurred, and my little doppelganger cries out in pain or ecstasy.

Cycle of Life, EUR 500. A naked man riding a bicycle through the canal district. His genitals – quite generously painted – droop over the seat and on his right bicep is a squiggled lion: my Scotland Forever tattoo. He rides towards a red-light window, where a caramel-skinned woman waves at the edge of the canvas.

As I stumble towards the next painting, I notice Dingo at the other end of the room. He holds a glass of champagne, and next to him, also quaffing champagne, is Morrow. I can't speak. I move towards them and place my hand on Dingo's shoulder, squeezing.

"Well, look who it is!" says Morrow.

"Findlay," says Dingo. He gestures to the painting in front of him, looks at me, then back at the painting.

I grip his elbow. “Where have you been all day?”

Dingo continues to stare at the painting.

Candy Stripes, EUR 500. It shows the Fin character naked, save for candy-striped pink-and-white leggings. All around him people frolic: they too wear the leggings, they too are naked, spidery pubic hair on display. Some of the characters are vaguely recognisable from my tapes. A vanilla-blonde woman – the Norwegian Temp? A leggy brunette with pierced nipple – the Belarussian prostitute? The Fin-character doesn’t look much like me beyond the brown hair, but the Scotland Forever tattoo is clear in unmistakable detail.

“You’re my fockin hero,” says Morrow.

Heels click on the polished floor behind me and I already know who it’s going to be. I swivel round to get the first words in.

Eva’s looking great in a one-piece black dress, a slender white ribbon tied in a bow around her neck. I lose the power of speech, and the initiative.

“Fin, I didn’t think it was right to invite you.”

“Really?”

Her expression is hard. “I’ve already sold three. I’ll give you a cut.”

I stare into her eyes.

She glances away. “This project was all about reinvention. I reinvented myself as a sexologist, and you lived a different life too.”

“But Eva, to do this...”

Anger flares in her face. "What are you talking about! Before you met me you were unfit, you drank too much, you had no sex. Look at you now!"

Morrow nudges me. "It's a fair point. She did a good job."

"And Strange Fruit? Zasha?"

She examines her champagne glass as if checking for lipstick stains. "I'm sorry. We needed to bring the project to an end, and I thought it would be best if you got scared off."

"Jesus Christ. So you asked her to beat me up?"

"Not beat you up. Just freak you out. She has a reputation for that."

"And you're playing the tapes. We had an agreement of confidentiality."

"I'm only playing my favourite bits: don't worry, I left the sensitive stuff out. Do you see or hear your name anywhere?"

I remember that one of the early tapes is about Ewan Semple's party and look at Dingo. He is surprisingly bright-eyed and fresh-faced, so I can only assume he's been spared that particular trauma. Eva turns away, air-kissing some new arrivals.

"And you, Dingo. Where were you today?"

He shrugs. "Hud a stinkin hangover so went for a walk. Ended up gaun tae the Anne Frank House n the Van Gogh Museum. Walked roond the canals, really fuckin lovely. Then I bumped intae McKirdy in Burger King n went tae the pub."

For the first time, I'm aware that people in the room are looking at me, some of them pointing. I notice the next painting.

Burned by Love, EUR 600. A self-portrait of Eva naked, one half of her body disfigured with smudged burns. Over her shoulder, amidst a deserted cityscape, standing on a rooftop, is the brown-haired man. At his foot lies another man, bleeding, beaten up.

More people crowd into the room, a sudden clamour. I recognise Lindy Grossman, wearing a purple sari-shawl, and behind her several of the Amoebas. I step closer to the wall and lean against the bare brick. My hand brushes the frame of the painting and I feel its solidity. The memories return: cycling through the summer night, hoping to find a new start, and stepping into the sport hall stink of sweaty feet and Deep Heat. Finding The Amoeba Group and a smiling Eva.

My fingers tighten on the frame of the picture. It wobbles in my grip. I hear Eva's laugh piercing the hubbub like an ice-pick and surprise myself by lifting the painting off its hook.

I throw it on the floor and leap directly onto the canvas. My feet burst the thin paper and I twist my heels into it, kick the rips open, rupture the image off its frame. The room is quiet. I step out of the wreck of canvas and swing a fist into another painting: my punch punctures a crude picture of shadow-men looming over a crumpled bed. Someone hisses their disapproval and as I turn, up for a fight, I see Eva calmly filming me on her mobile. With one swipe of my hand I knock it out of her grip and the handset bullets across the room and smashes into a tray of champagne glasses.

A blond man tries to manhandle me and I shoulder charge him away. I'm swearing at people, saliva dribbling down my chin.

A hand closes on my arm. Dingo. "We're going."

We push through the crowd, down the stairs and out the door.

Keizersgracht, and fresh air. I sit down on a cold stone step and bury my head in my arms. Dingo sits down next to me.

"Fucksake, min," Dingo says, placing a gentle hand on my shoulder. "Why did ye tell her aw that stuff? Why did ye no just keep yir mouth shut?"

I gaze out at the canal: melted reflections wobble on its surface.

"She told me it was therapy."

"Dinnae be an idiot, min."

A taxi creeps up the road and passes us, engine barely audible. We watch its taillights recede.

I sigh. "Anyway, why did you go AWOL today? I was crapping myself after everything you said last night."

"I shouldnae have reacted like that," says Dingo. "I've been a bit fucked up recently, keep hinkin I've wasted ma life. Thirty-five now. Halfway stage n whit have I achieved? Still in Cloudburn, still knockin roond wi laddies I kent at school." He fixes me in his stare. "Listen, Fin. The thing that scares me most is losin Ailsa n ma wee boy. I was wasted enough last night tae think it was about tae come true. Gilly pushed the right buttons."

I remember Gilly's words outside Strange Fruit and look at my boots. I also remember the hard pinch of the psycho-pimp's finger and thumb, his promise of staples.

"See," continues Dingo, "yill no want tae hear this, but Ailsa n me stayin faithful tae each other is one eh the few certainties in life. After whit happened tae her at Semple's party... well, she doesnae find it easy tae be intimate." His voice is quiet. "For like, ten years after it happened she couldnae physically have sex. Froze up. It was only when we got together that things changed. I'm shy that way so we're a good match. It took a year before sex worked for us." And then, his voice quieter. "Dinnae mention this tae the others, okay?"

I nod.

"If Ailsa was ever unhappy bein wi me, it would be cause I'm an idiot or dinnae listen. No because eh sex. I should eh telt Gilly tae fuck off, instead eh chuckin ma phone in the canal."

"You said it was over."

Dingo shakes his head. "I was wankered. That 10p mix was a bad idea. That n the beer, the whisky, n the dope."

I could sleep right here. Curl up on the stone and melt away.

Dingo grabs my arm and hauls me to my feet. "Cmon. Let's go for a quiet drink. We've had enough drama for one weekend."

Ten minutes later I'm sitting in my usual spot at the Nova Scotia, an untouched pint of eighty shilling in front of me. Dingo, Razor and McKirdy sit at the window table, drinking Cloudburn coffees and guffawing loudly. 'Boys from the County Hell' by the Pogues plays on the jukebox. The pub is unusually busy: Dutch students, a group of Canadian tourists and a gay Italian couple wearing matching yellow shirts.

The door batters open behind me and Morrow enters, carrying something bulky and square, wrapped in a black binbag. His face is bright red and he's having trouble breathing.

"Fin, I nicked it for ye!"

He whips away the binbag to reveal the candy-striped leggings painting. Dingo, Razor and McKirdy rise to their feet and applaud, and suddenly the whole pub joins in: cheers, jeers, glasses thumping on tables. Morrow removes the picture of Frank McAvennie from the wall and hangs *Candy Stripes* in its place. More clamour and cheering. Morrow stands on a chair and raises his arms.

"Ladies and Gentlemen, let's hear it for a new star of the art world... Mr Findlay McPhailure!"

MacBean turns up the music. The two gay guys go over for a closer look at the painting. The Canadians stumble over to the bar, goatee beards and whisky breath, and ask me what the story is. I reach for my pint. It looks like it's going to be a long night.

SUNDAY

Extracted from www.cloudburn.com

Today, Cloudburn Distillery still stands proudly overlooking the town. Eight thousand visitors pass through the gates every year. Our most popular attraction is in the main lobby, where the famed Bottle of Brotherhood is on display – a symbol of the folly of pride, but also of redemption.

And as for the curse? Well, some say the Fairies are still wreaking their revenge.

In September 1970, the rock star Jimi Hendrix went to a party in London. Witnesses reported him swilling from a bottle of Cloudburn before his girlfriend came to pick him up. Hendrix was discovered dead in the bed the following day, drowned in his own vomit.

In 1977, the light aircraft carrying the members of the rock group Lynyrd Skynyrd crashed into woodland in Mississippi, killing six. Recovered from the wreckage? A case of Cloudburn, miraculously intact.

In 1997, in the bar of an exclusive Paris hotel, chauffeur Henri Paul drank a couple of Cloudburns to wash down his prescription medicine before meeting his clients and driving out into the September night. Minutes later, he crashed his car into the wall of an underpass, killing himself and two of his passengers – including Diana, Princess of Wales.

Perhaps these are just co-incidences – who are we to say? After all, we wouldn't want to put you off enjoying Cloudburn Single Malt Whisky. Now that you know the full story – and if you are brave enough – uncork the bottle, inhale deeply until your nostrils tingle, and then pour yourself another healthy dram. Let's raise our glasses and drink to Cloudburn – a whisky to die for! *Slainte!*

One for the Road

An alien noise.

Trrrrrr.

I wake up. The duvet has rotated during the night, and only half-covers me: the room stinks of stale alcohol, and I'm wearing only one sock. For a moment I'm totally confused, then clarity arrives at the same moment as the two-day hangover.

Trrrrrr.

My doorbell. A eureka moment.

I pull on yesterday's clothes and rush down the stairs. On the first floor, Dingo is asleep on the sofa, safely encased inside the sleeping bag. I continue down the stairs to street level and fumble the door open.

Two cops.

A man and a woman. This is all my brain can process. A man and a woman, wearing police uniforms.

"Findlay McPhail?" says the man.

I nod.

"Can we come in?"

Upstairs, they sit down at the long table and I make coffee. Dingo rustles around on the sofa, groaning, like he's in the middle of an uncomfortable dream that two cops have arrived in the living-room of his future brother-in-law's apartment and want to question him about the destruction of two paintings. My hand shakes as I spoon instant coffee into three cups.

"You work for Cloudburn whisky, yes?" says man cop.

I set the steaming cups down on the table.

"Yes, that's right."

"We were advised by the Scottish police that you are the main contact for this brand."

I have no idea where this is going. They both look over at the drinks cabinet and the cluster of bottles and exchange a glance.

The woman cop speaks. "There has been a poisoning incident related to Cloudburn whisky."

My lungs shrivel.

"An old bottle. A very old bottle. We believe a colleague of yours is involved. A Mr Newt Sarkissian."

The cops are in the house for an hour. Dingo wakes up and sneaks upstairs. The cops tell me that Newt is under arrest on suspicion of poisoning three people. They ask if I know where he was last night – I tell them I have no idea, but as I'm saying this I remember leaving his sports bag in the basement room in Strange Fruit. They take my phone number and say they'll be in touch again when they have more information.

I close the door behind them and sit on the bottom step. Rain flurries on the frosted glass. I imagine the Bottle of Brotherhood in a police laboratory, a ticket tied to its neck, wax seal broken by careless hands. Dingo calls from above and I get to my feet and limp back up the stairs.

THE BIG DAY

Vows

I'm naked, ready to begin.

First, the socks. Woollen, a bit scratchy, pulled up to the knees. I get a flashback to the candy-striped leggings and blink it away. Next, the garters with green flashes. I snap them into place and adjust the elastic, until it's tight enough around my upper calves to ensure the socks stay up for the next fifteen hours, and tight enough to be a little kinky too.

Now for my favourite: the sgean dhu. I unsheathe it and admire the blade, surprisingly sharp. I stab an imaginary opponent. Here I stand in my boyhood bedroom, in a state of undress with a knife in my hand. I examine myself in the mirror and conclude that I'm recovering quite nicely. The nipple has scabbed up at last, and although painful to touch, feels like it won't require amputation. The bruising on my ribcage and thigh from the baseball bat is a cluster of grey and yellow spores – a bit shocking to look at, but far better than Monday's blue-black combo. I do a Bugs Bunny to reveal my front teeth, freshly capped by an Amsterdam dentist who quietly complained about foreigners not learning Dutch.

The bedroom is a mess. Since I vacated it eighteen years ago it's become a storage room, absorbing the overspill from the rest of the house, the sort of room that always has its door closed when visitors come to stay. But despite this inconvenience, behind all the stacks of boxes and bric-a-brac, my room remains preserved since 1991, like a missing child's. On one wall a sun-browned Pixies *Surfer Rosa* poster, on my desk the blue jotters in which, during that first summer at the distillery, I painstakingly wrote my tour-guide version of the Cloudburn Curse. A stack of university folders containing my lecture notes and essays on marketing and product design, the locked cabinet containing bundles of teenage letters, photos, newspaper cuttings. On top of a Cloudburn shipping case, a distillery polo shirt – I lift it up and it unfolds itself – faded, slightly mildewed, whitened with deodorant residue under one armpit. Another relic of that summer. As I replace it I notice the contents of the box: my wedding photos, packed away out of sight.

Ailsa and Dingo's wedding will be strangely similar to my own. Same venue, same ceilidh band, same photographer, two-thirds of the same guests. At this exact moment, the caterers will be organising the distillery function room: tables nudged into place, barrels of beer rumbled through the door, napkins folded, trays of food stacked in the walk-in fridge, arguments between the staff flaring up and dying away again. The head man of the ceilidh band sitting at his kitchen table, ticking through his checklist, imagining already the twiddle-diddle and drum-thump on stage, the hot-trot of feet on the floor. The photographer searching frantically for his battery charger. And the guests? No grandparents this time: sadly missed. The same gathering of the McPhail and Findlay clans, the cheery uncles and yakking aunties and cousins who like a drink just a bit too much. Razor: perhaps realising he should have dry-cleaned his kilt following the trip to Amsterdam, flaking off the chilli sauce and DNA samples with his thumbnail. McKirdy: regretting his trip to the Drookit Dug last night for a few warm-up pints, headache simmering, sudden realisation that he forgot to buy a gift making him hoot with shame. And eighty-odd other guests: showering, deodorising, lip-sticking, shaving, hair-brushing, hair-drying, daydreaming.

But no Gilly.

Last Sunday, after the cops visited, Dingo and I went for a long walk through the Jordaan, around Vondelpark and back into the centre again. He took photos in the bright autumn sunlight. After a late lunch in a nearby bruin cafe it was time to go to Centraal station. In the bar on platform 1 we met as agreed with the other distillery boys. Gilly sat in the corner hiding behind shades and baseball cap. Dingo tossed Gilly's bag at his feet and he nodded in acknowledgement. On platform 14, I shook their hands one-by-one. Except Gilly, who'd already got on the train. Razor whispered in my ear: "We'll be back for the Scotland game in March."

Da asked me last night what we'd done to Gilly in Amsterdam. "No been tae work aw week," he said. "His maw says he's lyin in bed, curtains closed, isnae touchin his food. Must eh come doon wi somethin bad."

A knock at the door. "Fin." My mother's voice.

"Aye, hang on, I'm bollock-naked."

"That's no way tae talk on yir sister's wedding day."

"Mum, did you want something?" I remain standing behind a stack of boxes, examining my white-socked feet.

"Aye. Dingo called. He'll meet ye at the end eh the road in half an hour. You n yir Da are tae tak him for a drink n calm him doon. Ailsa needs him tae be on form."

"Right you are. How's the bride?"

"Holdin up."

I reply loud enough for Ailsa to hear. "I thought she looked radiant half an hour ago, so she must be looking exquisite by now."

Ailsa shouts from her old room, something about her hair. Mum shouts back and clumps away down the hall. I smile. What I said was true: she looked terrific. It's up to me to prove we're related by at least being presentable.

I put the shirt on, the kilt, belt, and sporran. The picture in the mirror is improving, redesign gathering pace. It clicks that I should have put the shoes on before the kilt and spend five minutes struggling with the laces. Finally, I tighten the silver cravat around my neck, and shrug the jacket on. Redesign complete.

The door bumps open and Wee Calvin sticks his head in – togged up in a baby kilt, blond hair already messed up – and flings a tennis ball at me. It zips past my ear: he laughs and storms out again.

I check myself in the mirror one last time then go downstairs, humming 'A Scottish Soldier'. My father sits at the kitchen table, similarly kilted out, sipping at a mug of tea. He frowns in my direction.

"Yir in the news again the day." He slides the newspaper across the table:

ANTIQUE WHISKY CONFIRMED AS CAUSE OF DEATH IN BROTHEL POISONINGS

AMSTERDAM – Dutch police confirmed yesterday that a famous 115-year-old bottle of scotch whisky fatally poisoned three men in an Amsterdam brothel last Saturday.

Preliminary tests showed levels of toxicity consistent with potassium cyanide poisoning. Investigations are at an early stage, but it is believed the deaths were caused accidentally.

The bottle of whisky suspected to have caused the poisonings is thought to have originally been a gift between the brothers Edward and James Skene, original owners of the Cloudburn distillery, in the late 1920s. Known to whisky historians as The Bottle of Brotherhood, legend has it the bottle contained spirit from the first ever cask of Cloudburn whisky and was a gesture of reconciliation after thirty years of feuding between the two brothers. The bottle, once the centrepiece of the Cloudburn distillery visitor centre, was relocated to Amsterdam in 2007 when multinational company Stalwart purchased the brand, and took pride of place in a display cabinet in the company's marketing department until it was stolen at some point last week.

The presence of poison in the contents of this famous bottle has caused fevered speculation among whisky historians. Tavish Barclay, Cloudburn resident and author of the acclaimed whisky travelogue *Spirit of the Glens*, believes the poison was no accident.

"Cloudburn whisky is steeped in sinister and bloody history and this turn of events certainly adds further spice. Legend has it the original distillery owners were cursed by the Wee Folk for building the distillery on sacred fairy ground, and they certainly had their share of misfortune. Edward Skene was a skilled chemist and blender and it seems certain to me that he used his expertise to poison the bottle and bequeathed it to his brother James as a parting gift – a way to resolve their feud from beyond the grave. It certainly adds an intriguing new chapter to one of whisky's darkest tales."

A further twist in the case has been provided by the identities of the victims. All three men were known figures in Amsterdam's underworld, including the owner of the brothel, "Viking" Billy De Jong, 43, wanted by Interpol on three continents for people-trafficking and related offences.

Findlay McPhail, spokesperson for Cloudburn Single Malt Whisky, was unavailable for comment yesterday but stated earlier this week that Stalwart was co-operating with Amsterdam police and would provide a press release once the facts were clear.

I pour myself a strong cup of tea. Da looks at me for a moment, a shred of bloodied toilet roll sticking to his chin. "Will the facts ever be clear, son?"

"Facts never are."

He mutters and slurps his tea. "Ten minutes. Hopefully this fuckin shavin injury'll stop bleedin. Then we tak Dingo tae the Clachan. Razor n McKirdy are gaunny meet us on the way."

"Sounds good, Da." I read the article again and drink some tea. One phrase stands out – the bottle was stolen *at some point last week*. They don't know it was stolen on Saturday by the spokesperson for Cloudburn. Although the police probably still suspect Newt's involvement after finding his sports bag at the scene, which saw him taken in for questioning on Monday. I smile.

By the time I returned to my desk on Monday afternoon my inbox had over two hundred new emails, and the Cloudburn website over five thousand hits. The story of the Cloudburn poisonings had gone viral. The BBC's article was number 4 in their most read pages. Other, less well-informed reports had spread across the web. *GANGSTER PIMPS POISONED BY ANCIENT WHISKY. CURSE OF THE FAIRIES STRIKES AGAIN.* A raft of posts left on the Cloudburn messageboard. *Yr whisky rocks man. Fairies r real and this prooves it. Kill all perverts LOL.*

By Wednesday, I was struggling to take it all in.

The six thousand cases of Cloudburn gathering dust in the Paisley bond began to shift. Small orders, but unprecedented after three fallow months. The Stalwart demand team contacted me to suggest disgorging casks from the distillery stores to prepare for the Christmas rush. I received a call from the CEO of Stalwart, who instructed me that there would be extra marketing budget available for Cloudburn in the next three months. *We need a big push*, he told me. In the aftermath of the call I realised that the Cloud Nine re-branding and luxury hotel development was Newt's own secret work, probably his skewed vision for fast-tracking himself onto the Stalwart board. I drafted a carefully worded email to Newt, informing him of the upturn and extra budget, and took great pleasure in clicking *Send*.

Newt returned to work on Thursday – unshaven, brooding, growling. On a couple of occasions I caught him staring at me, as if I was a magic eye painting and a clear picture would jump out any second. But the picture will stay scrambled, I'll make sure of that. I might surprise him yet with a new direction for

Cloudburn. Maybe it is time to cut back on the troll and pixie shit. A proper fresh start in Amsterdam.

The doorbell rings. Da and I sit there without moving, waiting for the other one to move. It's not easy to get up when you're decked out in full kilt regalia. We are saved by Wee Calvin – he thunders down the stairs, howling like a yeti, and answers the door. A female voice. Da stands up and mutters.

"Da?"

He ignores me and moves away, and I hear the female voice again and realise why he's scarpering.

Kathleen stands in the doorway. Her hair is shorter, and she wears slender silver-framed glasses. Her swollen belly is barely contained in a blue maternity dress, one hand on her abdomen. Faint traces of her burns peek out at the wrist of her long-sleeved t-shirt. She smiles at me. "Hi Fin. Sorry to surprise you like this."

It's the first time I've seen her for almost two years.

At first I can't speak. Then I manage to get a few words out. "You look great, you know?"

Red-faced, she waves a hand in my direction. "I like the kilt."

"Have a seat."

"No, you're all right, I just came to drop this off." She lifts a glittery purple bag bulky with a wedding present.

"When are you due?"

"Six weeks."

"Are you living in Cloudburn these days?"

"No, just visiting my mum. Greg and I live in Perth."

Greg. Not Hamish?

She sees my confusion. “He’s a colleague. It all happened kind of quickly.”

“Are you married?”

She shakes her head. “I’m not religious anymore.”

Da hollers from the other room that it’s time to leave. I get up, and for a moment my kilt rumples and sticks out at the arse, peacock-like, before uncurling back into its normal shape. There is so much I want to say. She places the bag on the kitchen table and forces a smile. Our eyes meet and for a second the old Kathleen looks back at me – the Kathleen I knew back in the days of Nepalese curries, and bottles of wine in Edinburgh parks – and I realise that words are not needed.

She touches my arm. “It’s weird the way things turn out, right?”

I nod.

She steps away and raises a hand in an attempt at a casual wave. I watch as she moves down the hallway and out the front door. I can hardly breathe, but I’m surprised to feel happy – released from something, like after all this time I can finally let go. Maybe Eva had a point about my life being a patch of wasteland, overgrown with weeds and thornbushes. The ground is clear now, ready for something new to be built.

Da bundles back into the room and looks at his shoes. “I ken it’ll be difficult for ye the day, son.” He pats me on the shoulder. “The best medicine is tae see yir sister happy. And a good drink. Cmon.”

Out in the street, Kathleen’s red car is backing out of the driveway. She beeps once, and accelerates down the road, vanishing into the distance. Da makes positive noises about the good weather and we start off in the direction of the town.

When we turn the corner Da starts laughing. "Keek at him."

Up ahead, a kilted man sits on the bus stop bench with his head in his hands. "Gaun somewhere?" yells Da.

Dingo looks up and tries to smile. "Waitin for you pair eh fannies."

Da reaches into his jacket pocket. He takes out a silver hipflask and passes it to Dingo. "Cask strength, cut wi water fae the burn. Distilled 1975. The year Ailsa was born." He passes it to Dingo, whose eyes have filled with tears. "Dinnae you start greetin," Da warns.

Dingo drinks and passes the flask to me.

It's light in my hand, smooth to the touch, the pewter unmarked with any engravings or brandings. Whisky in its underpants. I raise the flask's thin neck to my mouth and a stream of Cloudburn trickles in. Da grabs it off me. "Easy lad, that's got tae last!"

Brambles, oatmeal, Thai chilli, seaweed. Glide and glow.

Da drinks and wipes his mouth. "Ye nervous, Dingo son?"

Dingo laughs too loudly. "Aye! Shitein it."

We resume our march towards the town centre. Kilt accessories clink and jangle as we advance – sporrans dance, fabrics rub together, kilts swing with each stride – and Dingo walks tall, shoulders back. On the other side of the street, a window slides up and a voice yells out: “Good luck Dingo, wee man!” Through the window of the newsagent, the proprietor Mohit gives a thumbs-up, his 10p Mix tray safely out of sight.

Up ahead at the war memorial, McKirdy and Razor wait for us. Razor plays an imaginary drum while McKirdy eats crisps. When we are within spitting distance they start yelling.

“Dingooooo!”

“The grooooom!”

“The condemned man!”

Dingo starts laughing and points at McKirdy’s legs. “Nice mini-kilt, Stevie.”

McKirdy’s kilt is a couple of inches too short and sits just above his skinny knees. We all laugh. McKirdy grumbles. “Gaunny kill ma fuckin brother – said it would fit me, the twazzock.”

I produce a small package from my sporran and hand it to him. McKirdy unwraps it and his face lights up.

“The fridge magnet! Yir a lifesaver, min. Ma maw’s bin chewin ma lugs aw week.”

Razor hooks an arm round Dingo’s neck and whispers secret words in his ear. They break, shake hands, and a passing car slows next to them. Dingo huddles in the window and chats to the driver.

“Fucksake, at this rate we’ll only have time for the one drink,” says Da.

“Cmon!” yells McKirdy. “Let’s hit the pub.”

As they bicker, I gaze up at the rocky crags of the Ochils looming above the town. After a year of Amsterdam’s blank horizon it’s a shock to see the sheer bulk of hills again. Already, the things I was blind to remind me of their existence. I look along the granite-edged outline of the hills until I spot the cairn, drop my vision down and there it is – the distillery's water source, at this distance just a crack in the stonework, and below that the untamed thicket of Fairy Glen. A flush of sunlight illuminates the slopes, and I smile: blue skies above Cloudburn, the curse broken at last.

A HUMBLE REQUEST

Dear Reader

Thanks for reading Amsterdam Rampant. I hope you enjoyed it. You might also like my second novel, The Devil's Chamber.

As an indie author I lack the marketing machinery of the giant publishing houses, and knowledge of my book spreads mostly through word of mouth. In order to build a profile, I need online reviews. So if you could please spare a moment, I would really appreciate a review on Amazon and/or Goodreads. Even if you didn't like the book, go ahead and share your views – any review helps me get better next time. I'm in this game for life!

Thanks, and all the best
Neil

PS. I've been blogging about the whole process of indie publishing, if you're interested you can read more here: http://ncocker.wordpress.com/

ACKNOWLEDGEMENTS

First of all, I owe the city of Amsterdam an apology.

I lived in Amsterdam for two years and worked in it for seven; for my money it is the most beautiful, unusual, insane, tranquil and inspiring city in the world. If you've never been, please go – enjoy the bruin cafes, parks, Thai food, canals, tolerance, and buzz. The sleazy bits are easily ignored. I am sorry if the novel encourages lazy stereotypes – the city is much much more than its dark corners. Fin's story came to me and I was a slave to it. Forgive me, my love.

Any writer who tells you their novel is their work alone is lying to you. I am indebted to many people for their generous help and advice.

Sean McNulty was there from day one and gave me numerous brilliantly detailed line edits – thanks for getting the book down to fighting weight (a great boxing metaphor that transfers beautifully to novel writing).

My former agent Jenny Brown was a huge believer in the book right from the beginning, and her energy and enthusiasm was always an inspiration. Thank you Jenny for your hard work and kindness – alas the big fish did not bite.

Mat Tate was another who helped me knock the book into shape. His wisdom and humour over curry and beers was a constant highlight of my days in Amsterdam.

Sinead Daly acted as my conscience. Her feedback was tough but helped me give the book more backbone.

Robert Glick persuaded me that any book about Amsterdam's dark side couldn't hold back. His advice freed me to follow the story to its dark heart and back out again into the light.

Mark Gallacher wrenched me away from overcomplicated back-story and navel gazing, and rewrote my synopsis like the killer editor he is.

Lexi Barbakoff helped me get back on my feet and dust myself off for another draft. Motherwell steel.

Gareth Goodall got me thinking about how to fine-tune the book's engine, how to recalibrate the chassis and get the story purring smoothly.

Alan Bissett persuaded me to stay true to a single voice (earlier versions had points of view of multiple characters). His advice gave the book its pace and punch.

Bob McDevitt gave me the feedback I needed to hear – sometimes a writer needs to kill his or her darlings. Many darlings tragically perished following Bob's advice, but the book was far better for it.

Adrian Searle of Freight Books was interested in publishing Amsterdam Rampant for a spell and we exchanged many emails and skyped. His feedback was honest and heartfelt, his advice excellent, and when he let me down gently it was with great grace and encouragement.

I met Zoe Venditozzi at the Dundee International Book Prize dinner and found out she had been a great cheerleader for the book during the competition. Her enthusiasm and encouragement gave me strength when the constant knockbacks were beginning to take their toll.

Thanks to my mum and dad for their constant encouragement and zest for life. Thanks too to my brother Ian whose beery Calvinist Zen put-downs have been a constant inspiration throughout my life.

Most importantly, thanks to my wife Anna. It's hard for a guy from the east coast of Scotland to express his emotions, but you are my best friend and I love you very much. Every time I look at you or listen to you I realise I am punching above my weight (another boxing metaphor). You have tolerated my writerly ego for ten years and the advice you gave me right back at the beginning was absolutely right (have the word Amsterdam in the title, get more of a love story in there) and I foolishly thought I knew better. You were right, as always. I'm a very lucky guy to have you.

Oh, and thanks also to you, dear reader. I hope it was an enjoyable ride. Sorry about the stapler.

Neil Cocker
February 2014

Printed in Great Britain
by Amazon

38623668R00150